SPLITSCREEN

SPLIT SCREEN

BRIDE OF THE SOUL-SUCKING BRAIN ZOMBIES

BRENT HARTINGER

HarperTempest
An Imprint of HarperCollinsPublishers

HarperTempest is an imprint of HarperCollins Publishers.

Split Screen: Attack of the Soul-Sucking Brain Zombies/
Bride of the Soul-Sucking Brain Zombies

www.harperteen.com

———————————————

Library of Congress Cataloging-in-Publication Data
Hartinger, Brent.
    Split screen / by Brent Hartinger. — 1st ed.
        p.   cm.
    Summary: Two books in one tell of sixteen-year-old friends
Russel, who is gay, and Min, who is bisexual, as they face separate
romantic troubles while working as extras on the set of a horror
movie.
    ISBN-10: 0-06-082408-5 (trade bdg.)
    ISBN-13: 978-0-06-082408-2 (trade bdg.)
    ISBN-10: 0-06-082409-3 (lib bdg.)
    ISBN-13: 978-0-06-082409-9 (lib bdg.)
    [1.   Homosexuality—Fiction. 2.   Bisexuality—Fiction.
3. Horror films—Fiction. 4. Motion pictures—Production and
direction—Fiction. 5. Actors and actresses—Fiction. 6. Family
life—Fiction.] I. Title.
PZ7.H2635Spl 2007   2006029872
[Fic]—dc22   CIP
                                                              AC

———————————————

Typography by Joel Tippie
1 2 3 4 5 6 7 8 9 10
❖
First Edition

For Jo Ann Jett (aka Mrs. O'Neal),
the opposite of a zombie in every way

Special thanks to Laura Arnold, Suzanne Daghlian,
Jennifer DeChiara, Elizabeth Duthinh, Robin Fisher,
Cara Gavejian, Lori Grant, Sarah Jellen,
Barbara Lalicki, Molly Magill, Margaret Miller,
Lisa Moraleda, Marcy Rodenborn, Patty Rosati,
Joan Rosen, Susan Schulman, Dina Sherman,
and Laura South-Oryshchyn.

CHAPTER ONE

BODY PARTS. A FLIER on one of the school bulletin boards was covered with little drawings of them: dismembered arms and feet and heads dripping with blood. They looked the way I felt. Disconnected.

My friend Gunnar had been the first to notice the flier. He'd beckoned to me and my other friend Russel on the other side of the hallway.

"They're filming a zombie movie in town, and they need teenagers to be extras, and isn't that *cool*, we should totally do it!" he said breathlessly. I hadn't seen him this excited since the night they left the gate unlocked at the sewage treatment plant.

I glanced at the words on the flier. ZOMBIES WANTED! it read.

Teenagers needed as extras for upcoming horror film, *Attack of the Soul-Sucking Brain Zombies*, to be produced in local area. Come let us turn you into gruesome, monstrous zombies!

The dismembered body parts surrounded these words.

My name is Min Wei, I'm sixteen years old, and I confess I adore monster movies. I was also keen on the idea of giving this movie some racial diversity, because, honestly, when was the last time you saw an Asian-American zombie? At that moment, however, I was in kind of a pissy mood.

"Aren't they kind of late for zombies?" I said. "Halloween was two weeks ago." It was currently the second week in November.

"They're *filming* the movie," said Gunnar. "Not releasing it."

Gunnar is the kind of person who somehow always manages to be wearing the wrong shoes. I would never say this out loud, but Gunnar might even have a mild form of autism, something like Asperger's syndrome. He is very intelligent but can become somewhat obsessive about things. He's also not so skilled at the human-interaction thing, if you know what I mean. However, he is still an extremely nice person.

"And what's a 'brain zombie'?" asked Russel. Russel is my best friend. He is quite adorable, but he doesn't know it, which just makes him that much more adorable. He is also very smart, but pretty emotional, always waving his hands all over the place. When he does that, he reminds me of Kermit the Frog, except with reddish hair. He can sometimes be exasperating, because he always has to see every side to everything. Still, he's a great guy, with possibly the world's biggest heart. Russel is gay, and his boyfriend's name is Otto.

"I know," I said to Russel. "Brain zombies? That doesn't even make sense."

"I'm sure it's explained in the script!" blurted Gunnar. "Look, do you guys want to do it or not? I know Em will." Em is Gunnar's girlfriend. I'd point out that she's really intelligent too, but then that makes three people in a row that I've called smart, and I accept that that might strain my credibility.

"I don't know," I said. I did want to be a zombie extra in the movie. For some reason, I just didn't want to come right out and say that.

Russel looked at me. "What's wrong?"

"Huh? Nothing."

The truth is, I knew exactly why I felt so disconnected.

Russel had a boyfriend, and Gunnar had a girlfriend. Ironically, I'm bisexual so I would have been okay with either a boyfriend *or* a girlfriend. I didn't have either one, however, so I was feeling a little excluded.

"This zombie thing could be fun," said Russel.

"Yes, maybe," I said.

"We'll all be together, at least," he said.

"No, we won't," I said. "Not really."

"Yeah, we will!" said Gunnar. "Why wouldn't we be?"

"Because people are always alone," I said. "Sure, we're 'together,' but not really. We all might be doing the same thing, being zombie extras on this movie set. But we wouldn't ever really know what the others are thinking or feeling. It'd be a completely different experience for each of us."

I know all this makes me sound like a crashing bore. As I said, I was feeling a little lonely, and this was just my not-so-desperate cry for help.

"Please," said Russel. "Zombie guts are zombie guts are zombie guts."

This was a reference to that Gertrude Stein poem, "A rose is a rose is a rose," which we'd studied in class. Like I said, Russel is smart. Funny too.

"Are they?" I said. "Zombie guts might mean one thing

to you, but something completely different to me. Even if we were always together, which we won't be, it wouldn't be the same experience at all. I bet you ten dollars that if we do this, we'll have completely different experiences."

"Yeah, but that doesn't mean—"

Suddenly Gunnar exploded. *"Enough with the boring philosophy talk!* Are we going to do the zombie movie or not?"

Russel and I both laughed. We couldn't make Gunnar suffer any longer, so we told him that of course we'd do the movie.

After that, Russel and Gunnar had to leave for class. I turned to go in the other direction when a voice said to me, "Nice hair."

It was Kevin Land, this big baseball jock. He's tall, dark, and handsome, if you go for that sort of thing. He'd been Russel's first boyfriend the year before, and their breakup had been an unpleasant one. For months afterward, I'd tried to help Russel mend the pieces of his broken heart. For weeks, he had sobbed in my arms, on my shoulder, and on various other body parts. Even before the breakup, however, Kevin had never been my favorite person. He's very popular, and like most people who are popular, he is a selfish weasel. I once asked him to stand up for this kid who was being bullied, and he'd been an absolute baby about it. In fact, Kevin's being such a selfish weasel is the reason why Russel had finally broken up with him.

Kevin's observation about my hair had to do with the fact that I'd recently given myself purple streaks. I could justify this by saying that I'd done it to express my individuality, but no, I'd really just wanted to shock people.

"Hey, Kevin," I said. Russel and Kevin didn't talk anymore, but I still acknowledged him, at least when Russel wasn't around. It's true that he's a selfish weasel, but I think some people have the opinion that I'm a little stuck up, so I try not to give anyone the cold shoulder.

"What's going on?" he said. "I thought I just saw you talking to Russel."

"They're filming a movie here in town," I said, gesturing to the poster on the bulletin board. "They need extras to be zombies, and Gunnar, Russel, and I are going to do it."

"Really?" Suddenly the poster had Kevin's attention.

"Wait," I said. "Why do you care?"

Kevin smiled enigmatically. "What makes you think I care?"

With that smug grin still on his face, he turned and sauntered on down the hallway.

Here's the thing. Like Gunnar, Russel, and Em, I'm

pretty smart. I hate to boast, but I was the smartest person even in GAT, which stands for "Gifted and Talented." I've always gotten a 4.0 without even trying, and I have no memory of anyone ever using a word that I didn't already know the meaning of. Even among other Asians, I stand out as unusually intelligent.

Given how supposedly smart I am, you'd think that it would have occurred to me before that very moment that there might be a reason *why* Kevin Land, Big Baseball Jock, still talked to me, Chow Mein Brain. It's true that I had dyed my hair purple, but when it comes to unpopularity at Robert L. Goodkind High School, a 4.0 GPA trumps purple hair any day.

Kevin obviously still liked Russel. Being Russel's best friend, I had all kinds of inside information on him. That's why Kevin kept talking to me. It was all so obvious.

Now I had given Kevin specific information on what Russel was going to be doing in the weeks ahead. Russel, however, had a new boyfriend now, Otto, and the last thing he needed was Kevin waltzing back into his life.

In other words, I may be really, really smart, but sometimes I can be pretty darn dumb.

*   *   *

Attack of the Soul-Sucking Brain Zombies was being filmed at a local high school, which had been closed for the year for renovations. Three days later, Russel, Gunnar, Em, and I went to an afternoon assembly at the auditorium of that high school, to find out exactly what was involved in our being zombie extras.

As we were sitting in the seats waiting for something to happen, Gunnar said, "Carrots and peas."

I stared at him. Like I said, sometimes he can be a little off.

"That's what movie extras are supposed to say to make it look like they're really talking," he went on. "They don't say real words, they just repeat the phrase 'carrots and peas' over and over again."

"Really?" said Em. "That's very interesting!"

Obviously, there is a reason why Em is Gunnar's girlfriend.

As the others kept talking, I looked around the auditorium. About forty teenagers had showed up for this meeting, mostly from other high schools in the area. I didn't see Kevin, which made me breathe a sigh of relief. Maybe he wasn't trying to ingratiate himself back into Russel's life after all.

I also didn't see very many girls. There were eight of us in all, including Em and me. They were all "aspiring model" types, just desperate for any chance to preen and "make love to the camera," even if they'd be making love as zombies. As for the guys, they appeared to be a bunch of computer gamers and role-playing aficionados, with lots of wispy beards and T-shirts with pictures of weaponry. None of this should have surprised me, but I was still disappointed.

Here's the thing. Part of the reason why I'd ultimately agreed to do this movie-extra thing was that I thought it might be a good way to meet someone. Most people really don't understand bisexuality. I hate it when people talk like bisexual people are indecisive, unable to make up their minds. It's not a question of being changeable, like a sea anemone, able to switch genders. I don't shift or waver or change, and I'm not on my way to anything other than being bi; I've always been bisexual, and I always will be. Why is that so hard for people to understand?

It's also not the case that I'm attracted to *all* guys and *all* girls—"anything that moves," as some people like to say. Like anyone, I'm only attracted to *some* people—some of them guys and some of them girls.

What kind of guys and girls do I like? Here's where it gets complicated. I hate the extremes: giggly girls with their catty backstabbing and frilly lace bras, and macho guys with their ridiculous swagger and stupid sex jokes. These people all seem like they're trying too hard. I like people who are comfortable in their own skin. I also like it when someone is confident and decisive and bold and generally just not afraid of making some waves in life.

Listen to me. I have this specific list of requirements for a boyfriend or a girlfriend, like I'm this fantastic catch myself.

All this was moot, of course. They say that romance comes when you least expect it. I'd come to this meeting expecting it, so it wouldn't come. Or would it? Since I knew that romance only comes when you least expect it, and I was expecting it, ironically I was no longer expecting it. So maybe romance would come. Thinking that, however, meant I was expecting it again.

Sometimes life is so confusing.

Finally, two young guys walked out onstage. They introduced themselves as the producer and director of *Attack of the Soul-Sucking Brain Zombies*. They talked a little bit about the movie itself, about how they saw it as both a satire of and homage to other monster movies. When it comes to movies, talk like this makes me nervous, because it always seems like someone is trying to make excuses for character clichés and formulaic plots.

As the director and producer talked, another girl took a seat on the aisle over to my right. She was tall but didn't slouch; had blond hair, but had pulled it back into a simple ponytail; and had smooth skin, but wore only lip gloss. Her navy jacket looked like something from the Civil War—Union, not Confederate—complete with brass buttons in front and actual epaulets on the shoulders.

The producer kept talking, but I wasn't listening anymore. I was staring at the girl on the aisle. Maybe it was the epaulets, but I couldn't keep my eyes off her.

Finally, they asked us if we had any questions. Gunnar, of course, made an inquiry about fake blood.

I kept staring at the girl in epaulets.

This time, however, she looked right at me, and smiled. Had she seen me staring at her all along? The overhead lights were still on, so it was pretty likely that she had.

Panicking, I turned back to the stage. For some reason, I felt like I should pretend I had been listening to the producer all along, so I raised my hand and asked how much we'd be paid.

Shortly thereafter, the producer and the director gave us a demonstration of the special effects they'd be using in the movie. It was all very impressive, and the audience loved it.

However, I was still thinking about the girl in the epaulets, and what exactly that smile meant. Could it be she was interested? Of course that meant I was back to "expecting" a romance, which meant it definitely wasn't going to happen.

We had at least one thing in common. She had epaulets; I had purple hair. If this had been a game show, the category would be Things That People Stare At.

I made the decision to talk to her on the way out of the auditorium. "It's going to take some work to turn *you* into a zombie," I would say, flirting brazenly. She would blush, flustered, but then say how much she liked my purple hair. Only now would I comment on her epaulets, since that was the obvious thing, and we would go from there. She might even invite me out for coffee. I had come alone in my own car, so it was conceivable that I could go.

Finally, the meeting was over, and we all stood up to leave. I turned toward the girl in the epaulets, to sort of maneuver my way toward her.

I didn't see her. I did spot Kevin Land, however. He had been sitting in the back row. I knew in an instant that he was waiting there to do to Russel what I was trying to do to the girl in the epaulets—to "accidentally" run into him. This was the last thing Russel needed. I knew how much he missed Kevin.

This was entirely my fault. Why had I been so stupid as to tell Kevin that Russel and I were doing this movie? I needed to stop this from happening.

"Russel?" I said. "Wait! Let's go out the other way!"

I don't think he heard me. I grabbed him by the jacket, but it was too late. He'd already entered the river of people rolling toward the exit. The current was too strong, and I lost my grip on him. There was no way to stop him from running into Kevin now. I decided to follow close behind to see if I could minimize the damage.

Russel saw Kevin almost immediately.

"Kevin?" he said. I couldn't help but notice how pleased he looked.

"Kevin!" I said. I didn't disguise the annoyance in my own voice.

"Hey, Russel!" said Kevin. "Hey, Min." He wouldn't look at me, probably due to the fact that I was scowling at him from right behind Russel.

"Uh, what are you doing here?" Russel asked him. As if I didn't know.

"Well," said Kevin. "I wanted to be a zombie."

"Is that *right*?" I said pointedly. I was more aware than

ever that Kevin is exactly the kind of macho guy I detest: strong on the outside, but with absolutely no backbone, at least not when it comes to anything real.

"Yeah," said Kevin. "That was pretty cool, what they did, huh?" He meant the display of special effects that the producer and director had had up onstage.

"Huh?" said Russel. "Oh, yeah, it was. So you came here to be a movie extra too?"

"Yeah," said Kevin. "I saw that poster in the hallway, and I thought it looked really interesting."

"What a *coincidence*," I said. I turned my back on him. "Russel, we should go." The river of people had pulled Gunnar and Em away from us and had probably already deposited them in the parking lot.

"Yeah," said Russel. "Sure. Well," he said to Kevin. "See you."

I prodded Russel back into the flow of exiting people, but it had lessened to a mere trickle now.

"Hey, Russel?" called Kevin. Before I could stop him, Russel looked back. "We should get together sometime," Kevin went on. "Just to talk."

"I mean it!" I said to Russel, firmly. "We really have to go."

Before either of them could say anything else, I grabbed Russel by the jacket and started dragging him away.

Gunnar and Em were waiting for us outside. I also saw the girl in the epaulets, on the other end of the campus— so far away that I'd never catch up to her now.

I guess that secretly I'd been expecting something to happen after all.

CHAPTER TWO

THIS IS THE PART where I'm supposed to complain about my family.

I wish I could. There are few greater joys in life than finishing a test before anyone else and complaining about one's family. The truth, however, is that my family is pretty decent.

I love my mom. She's one of those people that, whenever she's around, you have the feeling that things can't ever get too out of hand. It's hard to pin down exactly why. I think it's because she's verbal, but not pretentious; she's thoughtful, but not neurotic; and she's organized, but not rigid. Her fatal flaw is her taste in clothing, which is just inexcusably bad.

She has a Ph.D. in education and is always doing

research on various teaching methods. Not surprisingly, I ended up her best subject. Free school, homeschool, unschool, Montessori school, progressive school—you name it, I've done it. Finally, when I turned fourteen, I put my foot down and said I wanted to go to plain old public school. To her credit, she said okay.

Her parents were born in China, but she was born in the United States. Even so, she was raised to be very much the dutiful Chinese daughter, always deferential and attentive, especially to men. To hear her tell it, she was. Around the time she turned thirty, however, she realized that she'd been a fool, that you didn't get anywhere in the United States by being deferential and attentive, especially to men. In the United States, you got ahead by being loud and aggressive. She's always saying that in America, it's not so much what you say, but how you say it.

By the time I came around, my mom was determined that I not make the same mistakes she had. So from a very early age, she always encouraged me to speak up. Supposedly, she wouldn't feed me until I cried at a certain volume—sort of the Ferber Method in reverse.

I think she created a monster. Sometimes I wonder if my mom regrets raising a daughter who has a definite opinion about everything and who, unfortunately, doesn't always know when to shut up. I've certainly horrified enough of our relatives.

My dad, for example. He is much more traditional. He was born in China and didn't come over to the United States until he was seven years old. He's always shaking his head whenever I say or do something shocking, but he never actually criticizes me. The truth is, I think he's secretly proud of the fact that I stand up for myself. It's like I get to say and do all the things he never let himself say or do.

He's a Ph.D. too, but he prefers to teach rather than do research. He's also soft-spoken and mild-mannered, but absolutely uncompromising. If I get my candor from my mom, I get my sense of ethics from my dad. He's the kind of person who always corrects the checker for undercharging him—even if it's just a dollar, even if the checker is obviously incompetent, and even if it means my dad is going to be late. He's a big believer in personal sacrifice, and I am as well. He often says, "If ethics were easy, everyone would have them." If my dad gets embarrassed by my mom for being outspoken, she gets frustrated with him for being so obstinate. According to her, the world will not end if she lies and tells the waitress that one of her kids is a year younger than she really is, so we can still order off the damn children's menu.

Finally, there's my sister, Lei. She's six, so there's not a lot to say. She likes Barbies. This drives both my parents absolutely bonkers, which I think is to their credit, but what can they do?

I am named after my father's mother, Grandma Min, who now has Alzheimer's and who lives in an Alzheimer's unit a couple of miles away. I used to be jealous that my name wasn't Heather or Catherine, like the other American-born Chinese girls I know. Now, however, I appreciate that my name is a little unusual.

Earlier this year, I came out to my parents as bi. As I'd expected, they'd experienced some difficulty at first. Still, my parents pride themselves on their education, and on the very idea of education. Once they got over their initial distress, they went out and educated themselves. Despite what some people try to pretend, the research on sexual orientation is clear and overwhelming: it's a characteristic, not an illness; the feelings are involuntary, not freely chosen; and it's not changeable. My parents had learned that, and they'd immediately come around.

Finally, while still on the subject of my family, I'd like to take a moment and make fun of all things Chinese. Because I am Asian myself, I can do that, and no one can call me racist.

So here's to all the vinyl tablecloths, and to a hundred different Tupperware containers in the fridge, each containing one little bite of food. Here's to school supplies given as Christmas gifts, and to mothers who can't just order what's on the menu. Here's to too many damn dragons, and dads who think they can fix anything, but only end up making it worse.

There. Now that that's out of the way, we can move on with the story.

For as far back as I can remember, my mom and I have had tea together whenever I got home from school. I should probably think it's silly. After all, I am sixteen years old. Most kids my age barely even talk to their parents, much less have tea with them. The truth is, I kind of like having my mom fuss over me for a few minutes every day. The fact that we have Ding Dongs with our tea doesn't hurt.

The afternoon of the zombie meeting, my mom and I sat at the kitchen table while we waited for the tea to steep. It isn't a tea ceremony or anything, but it is true that we never start talking until the tea is done. Mom always uses fresh tea too, never tea bags. She can actually be quite snobby about this; she refuses to even drink the tea at most restaurants.

Finally, my mom poured two cups, one for her, one for me. According to tradition, you're supposed to drink the tea in three gulps, but we never do.

"So," said my mother. "How was your day?" She was wearing paisley with plaid. It looked like a pair of drapes threw up on her. Still, I'd long since learned that it was futile to point out things like this.

"Oh, it was fine," I said. It was technically still the afternoon, so we were drinking green tea. I explained about the meeting for the zombie movie, but I didn't mention the girl in the epaulets.

"That sounds like fun," said my mom.

"Yes, I think it will be."

I sipped my tea while my mom nibbled on her Ding Dong, watching me.

Finally, she said, "Min, what's wrong?"

"Wrong?" I said. "There's nothing wrong. Why do you think something's wrong?"

"You seem sad."

"No. Not at all."

"You're lonely, aren't you?"

I kept sipping my tea. I refused to affirm or deny the accusation.

"I remember what it was like," said my mom wistfully.

"More than anything in the world, I wanted a boyfriend." Her eyes met mine. "Or a girlfriend!" she added quickly. "Not that I wanted a girlfriend. Just that it's okay if you want a girlfriend too."

This is a good example of how much my parents had come around regarding my sexual orientation.

"I guess so," I said noncommittally.

My mom studied my hair. "Did I tell you how much I like the purple?"

I sighed. "Yes, Mom. About a hundred times." I didn't regret dyeing my hair, but it would have been a lot more satisfying if my mom had been horrified, like any normal parent.

"Well, I do," she said. "It really expresses your individuality."

"Thanks," I said, but individuality or not, I still wasn't going to tell her I liked her pants.

That Saturday, we had our first day of work on *Attack of the Soul-Sucking Brain Zombies*. We had an 8 A.M. makeup call at the school where they were filming. I wasn't thrilled to go that early, but in my family of workaholics, I'd long since been transformed into a morning person whether I liked it or not.

Climbing out of my car in the parking lot, I spied Kevin nearby.

"You!" I said, approaching him like a storm.

"What about me?" he said. He looked taken back, to say the least.

"What are you *doing* here?"

"What do you mean? I wanted to be a zombie. What's wrong with that?"

"That is not why you're here, and you know it!"

"It is so!"

"Kevin!"

"What?"

"What, are you stalking him?" I said.

"Who?"

"You know who!"

"Min! No, I'm not stalking him."

"Look," I said, lowering my voice. "I'm warning you that—"

Right then, Gunnar drove up with Em and Russel. They piled out, and we all acknowledged one another. I obviously couldn't talk to Kevin anymore, so I just stood there glaring at him. Once again, he would not look me in the eye.

As we walked inside, everyone was talking, but I wasn't

listening. I was thinking about Kevin. What was he up to? It didn't make any sense. The exact reason he and Russel had broken up all those months ago was because Russel had come out to the whole school but Kevin hadn't. He'd been too petrified about becoming even slightly less popular. He'd actually teased Russel for being gay, to draw attention away from himself. After that, Kevin had even had the temerity to want the two of them to keep seeing each other, in secret, but Russel had said no. I absolutely supported him. I'd tried a relationship in hiding once, with my first girlfriend, Terese, and it had been a complete catastrophe. It was impossible. It required that you be two completely different people, and in high school it's hard enough just being *one* person. I would never make that mistake again, and I wouldn't let Russel do it either.

Kevin knew all this, so what was he thinking now?

A couple of production assistants were waiting for us at a table just inside the door. They collected the release forms that we'd had to get signed by our parents and presented us with plastic numbers, the kind you get at a hardware store to put on your mailbox. I was number six.

More extras were arriving all the time, so one of the assistants led us to what they called the "hospitality suite," which was really just the school cafeteria with some boxes of doughnuts and bagels, trays of fruit, and jugs of orange juice spread out on one of the tables.

There was only one teenager in the hospitality suite before us: the girl in epaulets. She was wearing a different jacket now, though, one that didn't have epaulets.

I was so surprised, I dropped my plastic number. I don't know why I hadn't expected to see her again, but I really hadn't.

Russel reached down and picked it up for me. "Oops," he said. "You dropped this."

I didn't answer. I was watching the Girl Who Had Formerly Worn Epaulets, standing all by herself near the doughnuts. Apparently, she'd come alone. Right then, I decided I wanted a doughnut too.

I sidled up beside her and reached for a napkin. I could see her perfect profile, not to mention the fact that she wasn't wearing makeup.

She immediately turned to me. "Hey there," she said. "So you want to be a zombie, huh? That'll be a challenge."

Wait, I thought. That was way too similar to the line I'd been going to say to her, about how hard it would be to turn her into a zombie. I couldn't say it now.

"Oh," I said instead. "Thanks." Or did she mean something about my being Asian?

"Nice hair," said the Girl Who Had Formerly Worn Epaulets.

"Thanks," I said again. At this point, the plan had been for me to comment on her epaulets, but she wasn't wearing them anymore.

This was stupid. I was interested in this girl. Why couldn't I talk to her?

"Carrots and peas!" I blurted. It was the only thing I could think of. That said, we *were* here to be movie extras, and Gunnar's account of what extras supposedly say in the background *was* a fun piece of trivia.

"Pardon me?" said the Girl Who Had Formerly Worn Epaulets.

Before I could explain what I was saying, the production assistant stuck her head back into the classroom.

"We're ready for numbers one and two," she said.

The Girl Who Had Formerly Worn Epaulets looked down at her number. "Oh, that's me. Well . . . bye." She smiled at me and strode over toward the production assistant.

Wait! I wanted to say. I needed to explain what I meant when I'd blurted "carrots and peas." Because if I *didn't* explain, she was going to think I was stupid or weird—she might even think I had a mild case of Asperger's syndrome, like Gunnar.

Before I could say another word, she was gone.

It was destiny. Me and the Girl Who Had Formerly Worn Epaulets were destined never to talk.

"All right," said the production assistant to the Girl Who Had Formerly Worn Epaulets. "And two? Who's two?"

No one moved.

"Come on, folks, we're on a tight schedule here."

I looked down at my own number at last. It said "two," not "six." When I'd dropped mine and Russel had picked it up, he must have given me his number by mistake.

"Oh!" I said stupidly. "I'm two!"

"Well, come *on*," said the assistant impatiently.

A couple of people tittered, but I didn't care. I still had another chance to talk to the Girl Who Had Formerly Worn Epaulets. Maybe I'd even be able to explain what in the world I had meant by "carrots and peas."

They led us to a classroom, which had been set up as the wardrobe department. Once there, the costumers took one look at us and said, "Cheerleaders." Then they asked us our sizes.

We told them, but then I added, "I never really thought of myself as the cheerleader type before."

"Don't have any choice," said one of the costumers. "We desperately need cheerleaders for the first scene."

"Oh," I said. "Really scraping the bottom of the barrel, huh?"

The Girl Who Had Formerly Worn Epaulets laughed.

The costumer looked up at me and smiled. "Sorry, that came out wrong. I just meant we only had six female extras show up today. You'll make a great cheerleader." She tousled my hair. "Hey, love the streaks."

"Thanks," I said.

"But we'll probably have to put you in a wig for filming. Cheerleaders and purple hair don't really go together."

"Yes," I said. "That's why I did it."

They gave us costumes in our sizes, then sent us behind this partition to undress.

"Can you believe it?" I said to the Girl Who Had Formerly Worn Epaulets. "Cheerleaders?"

"Hey, watch it," said the girl mischievously. "I *was* a cheerleader."

"No way!"

"What?" she said. "You don't think I have the bod?" By now, she had undressed down to her underwear.

She *definitely* had the bod. She was lean and athletic, and part of me hated her perfect bod. To make matters worse, she was wearing a pink thong. I've never worn one. I've never even touched one. The whole idea of a thong just seems so preposterous.

She also shaved her legs and wore toenail polish. I shave my legs every now and then, but not without cutting myself, and I'd never worn toenail polish in my life. Clearly, this girl liked conforming to our culture's arbitrary standard of female beauty. Even so, that didn't make it any less attractive.

All of this seemed contradictory to me. She didn't wear makeup, but she wore toenail polish? She wore that funky Union jacket, and also a thong?

In any event, I'd clearly been wrong to be interested in The Girl Who Had Formerly Worn Epaulets—not just because she was way out of my league, but because she was undoubtedly not into girls. The fact that she'd been a cheerleader and wore a thong definitely trumped the lack of makeup and the funky Union jacket—just like my 4.0 GPA trumped my purple hair.

I turned away to undress, mostly because I didn't want her comparing her body to mine. "When exactly were you a cheerleader?" I asked.

"In the seventh grade," she said. "That young, it really *is* about leading cheers. Well, sort of."

I relaxed a little. She hadn't been a cheerleader since

the seventh grade? Maybe that didn't trump everything; maybe she *was* into girls. So that meant that all I had to worry about was the fact that she was still way out of my league.

"Did you do the whole pom-pom thing?" I asked.

The Girl Who Had Formerly Worn Epaulets laughed. "Yup!"

"Did you have little mini pom-poms on your shoes? Pink headbands and yellow scrunchies?"

"Unquestionably."

"The closest I've ever come to cheerleading is . . ." I thought for a second. "Well, now!" I was dressed, so I turned around to show her how I looked. "Well?" I said, spreading my arms.

"Very nice! And me?" Now she modeled for me.

"Even nicer," I said, and it sounded just as suggestive as I'd intended. Finally, I was back to being my usual, forthright self.

From wardrobe, they led us to another classroom, which was the makeup department. The artists there gave me a black wig, and caked enough makeup on me and the other girl to make us look exactly like teenage girls wearing too much makeup. The Girl Who Had Formerly Worn Epaulets and I chatted the whole time.

She was witty and quick, and even though we hadn't talked about anything important, I was 99 percent certain that her politics were like mine, frighteningly liberal.

It wasn't until after they'd led us back to the hospitality suite to wait for the filming that I realized that I still didn't know her name.

"Oh!" I said. "I'm Min."

"Leah," said the girl.

"Hi."

"Hi." She thought for a second. "Hey, you maybe wanna get some dinner after this thing is all over?"

CHAPTER THREE

Yes, I wanted to get dinner with Leah!

I had been quite looking forward to this movie shoot.

Despite what I'd told Russel and Gunnar, I had been eagerly anticipating being an extra, seeing how things were done on an actual movie set. Once Leah and I had made our plans, however, our dinner was suddenly all I could think about.

The strangest thing about making movies is how different everything behind the camera is from what's in front of the camera. It's like two completely different worlds. This makes sense, of course, since what's behind the camera and what's in front of it serve such different functions.

The first shot took place in the school hallway near the

front doors. In front of the cameras, it looked like a typical, if idealized, high school hallway. Neatly lettered posters hung from the walls, and teenage extras dressed as students milled around in front of the rows of freshly painted lockers.

Behind the camera, however, it looked like an explosion at Circuit City. Technicians in headphones twisted dials on black consoles while other technicians adjusted these banks of lights and the white panels used to reflect and focus the lights. Cables and cords snaked everywhere. The whole chaotic mess reminded me of a bees' nest, except that the worker bees—the technicians and assistants—were swarming around not one, but two queens: the director and the movie camera itself, which was black and bulky and resting on a dolly.

The two worlds even seemed to *smell* different: on the high school side with the student extras, it smelled like teen grooming products—perfumes and hairspray on the girls and body spray on the guys; on the side with the lights, cameras, and technicians, it smelled like stale coffee and sweat.

We started shooting the first scene. The main character, a teenager named Brad, comes to his new high school for the first time, but the other students tease him for wearing the wrong color socks. We extras just promenaded back and forth in the background.

"Good!" said the director when we were finished. "Let's set it up again, folks!"

While everyone moved back into place for a second take, the director had a series of little conversations, first with his assistants, then the producer, then the actors.

While we waited, I glanced over at Leah. She was deep in discussion with some of the other cheerleaders.

She saw me and smiled, but I looked away. I happened to see Kevin talking to Russel, but Russel looked angry, which was good, so I figured it was best if I just kept my distance.

Finally, the director was ready for us again, and we shot the same scene for the second time.

In fact, we kept filming that same scene, again and again, all morning. I'd had no idea that film work involved so much repetition.

"There are all kinds of things to consider," said Gunnar, coming up to me at one point.

"What?" I said, confused by his statement.

"The lighting, the sound, the performances of the actors, even the extras," he said. "If one of us looks right at the camera, they have to shoot the whole thing over again. That's why they're doing all these different takes. It's a lot of work to set these shots up, so they want to make absolutely certain they get everything just right before they move on."

"Oh," I said. "That makes sense." I was distracted; I couldn't help but notice that Leah was still chatting with the other cheerleaders. Someone must have just said something hilarious, because she was laughing uproariously. For a second, that seemed strange, but then I remembered how the girls she was talking to weren't necessarily actual cheerleaders; we were all just dressed up for the movie.

Russel joined us. "So what are you doing tonight?" he asked me.

"Tonight?" I said. "Nothing much." For some reason, the idea of telling Russel and Gunnar where I was going made me uneasy. I didn't know if this "dinner" with Leah was a date or not, but telling them about it seemed like a sure way to jinx it, of "expecting" something to happen when I should have been least expecting it.

We must have shot that scene in the hallway fifteen times. By the time we broke for lunch, I was convinced that Leah had forgotten all about our going to dinner, or at least changed her mind.

On our way back to the hospitality suite, I saw she was finally by herself again, so I couldn't resist stepping up next to her.

"We still on for dinner?" I asked.

"Unquestionably!" she said. "There's this great little Ethiopian place near here. You ever had Ethiopian food?"

I replied that I hadn't, but that I thought the idea was a good one. She told me where the restaurant was.

"Why don't we just meet at the restaurant right after the shoot?" I said.

"Sure," said Leah.

The rest of the day was a blur—but a very, very slow blur.

That night, I met Leah at the restaurant. It was just a little hole in the wall, with linoleum tabletops and macramé wall hangings. Someone had knocked toothpicks all over the floor. The fluorescent lights hummed, and the air smelled of garlic and sour milk.

Leah was waiting for me just inside. "I know it doesn't look like much," she said. "But trust me, the food's really great."

We claimed a table, and the waitress—an extremely bored twelve-year-old girl who was clearly the daughter of the owner—gave us these oversize, laminated menus. I'd had a lot of different cuisines in my life, but this one was new even to me.

"You want me to order?" said Leah. "They serve it kind of family style anyway."

Here's the thing: I'm a vegetarian. For some reason, however, I was reluctant to tell Leah that. That's really not like me. I usually don't have a problem telling people my opinions. I guess I was hesitant because I really wanted Leah to like me.

"How about the vegetarian combo?" I suggested, keeping my eyes locked on the menu. "That looks good."

Leah looked up. "You a vegetarian?"

She was going to learn I was a vegetarian sooner or later. It's not like I was going to change my whole way of living, not to mention sacrifice my principles, just to get together with her. As a result, I said, "Yes."

"Yeah?" said Leah. "Me too! And the vegetarian combo was exactly what I was going to order."

"You're a vegetarian?" I said, surprised, but very pleased.

She nodded and fiddled with the sugar packets.

"For how long?"

She plucked a napkin from the dispenser. "Well, I wouldn't call myself a *strict* vegetarian."

"How so?"

"Sometimes I eat meat."

I laughed. "Yes, that's not what I call a strict vegetarian either!"

Leah laughed too; I had meant for her to be in on the joke. "I just get so sick of eating nothing but French fries."

"And salad," I said.

"God, yeah! I'm so sick of salad. With that horrible low-fat Italian dressing. That's the worst."

The "waitress" came and took our order. Then Leah asked me, "So how come you're vegetarian?"

This proved that Leah knew something about vegetarians after all. There are so many different reasons not to eat meat. I also appreciated that she didn't say "I'd heard that your kind doesn't eat a lot of meat," which people have actually said to me before.

"Animal cruelty," I said. "I like meat. I'd eat it in a minute if they didn't raise it the way they do. People always say that it's natural to eat meat—you know, that cavemen ate meat, and all that. Sure, and I agree. But cavemen didn't keep their pigs in cages so small they can't move, and grow them so fat that they can't stand up on their own, and feed them ground-up other animals for food. Anyone who's ever owned a pet knows that animals can feel pain and fear." I thought for a second, then winced. "So you eat meat, huh?"

Leah laughed again. "Don't worry. You're absolutely right, and I know it. I should be a lot better."

I may be opinionated, but I'm not an idiot. I decided to change the subject.

"What made you want to do this zombie movie?" I asked.

"Oh, I just love monster movies," said Leah. "I saw the sign in our hallway at school, and I just knew I had to do it."

"No way," I said. "You really love monster movies? So do I!"

"Yeah, but really only a certain kind of monster movie. I mean, they have to take it seriously, you know? I hate it when you get the sense that the filmmakers don't really believe it, like they're just in love with the special effects. Because monsters aren't 'real,' you now? But it *is* a monster! How much more serious can it be? It's like that scene in *The Ring* when the main character hears the TV on, and she runs into the family room and sees that her son has just watched the evil videotape that means the ghost is going to come for him in seven days. Sure, maybe that can't happen in real life—but it's happening in the movie! They take it seriously, so how can *you* not take it seriously?"

I agreed with everything Leah had said, even about that scene in *The Ring*. I couldn't remember the last time I had completely agreed with everything *anyone* said.

"What's your favorite monster movie?" I asked.

"God, there are so many," said Leah. "But my favorite is probably *Invasion of the Body Snatchers*. The original, of course. One, it's genuinely creepy. But two, there's this sense that the world really is coming to an end. And you believe it! I mean, they never really explain how those whole pod-creatures work—you fall asleep, and they somehow form your body double? I mean, *huh*? But it doesn't matter. The filmmakers and the actors obviously really believe it, so you do too. And it's really scary!"

Right then, our food came, which was a big round tray covered with a gigantic, bubbly pancake. Directly on top of the pancake were mounds of various dishes—stewed lentils, collard greens, garbanzo beans, split peas, and some kind of cabbage and carrot concoction.

"Wow," I said.

"That's the *injera*," explained Leah, meaning the pancake thing. "Some people think it's too sour, but I love it."

"Oh," I said. I glanced around the tabletop. "I think I need a fork. And a plate?"

"You eat with your hands," said Leah. She reached out

and tore off a piece of the *injera*. Then she used it to scoop up some of the lentils and popped the whole thing in her mouth.

"Oh," I said. I felt stupid, and I thought about the times when I was younger and I'd had non-Asian friends over for dinner, but forgotten to get them a fork.

"Watch out for the cabbage thing," said Leah with her mouth full. "It's *spicy*. But damn, this is yummy."

I tore off some of the *injera*. I'd expected it to be warm, but it wasn't. I popped it in my mouth.

"Oh!" I said. "It's good!" I didn't say it, but it was also fun eating with my hands.

"Back to monster movies," said Leah. "What's *your* favorite?"

I thought for a second, but not just about monster movies. I was trying to decide how to answer. What if I mentioned a movie Leah hated? That was a stupid thought, of course. If I answered, either Leah would like what I had to say, or she wouldn't. Either way, she would be getting to know the real me, which was the only thing I had to offer her.

"*Aliens*," I said. "That's my favorite monster movie by far. One, because it has Sigourney Weaver. What more do you need? But two, because it has my favorite movie line of all time. It's at the end of the movie, and Sigourney has just moved heaven and earth to save her surrogate daughter from the aliens—only to discover that the alien queen has secretly stowed away on board their spacecraft and is now hovering over the girl, about to kill her anyway. So Sigourney suddenly steps out of that storeroom strapped into that awesome power-loader forklift contraption, and she says to the alien queen: 'Get away from her, you *bitch*!'"

Leah busted up. "Oh, God, I *love* that line! And I love that forklift thing—it's all set up so perfectly earlier in the film! God, that movie is a *classic*!"

We kept laughing and talking—both of us now. The overhead lights still hummed, and the smell of sour milk was stronger than ever, but I was having an incredible time.

In other words, it sure felt a lot like a date to me.

Still, *was* it a date? I had no way of knowing; I'd never actually been on one before. I had only ever met my one other girlfriend, Terese, in this abandoned warehouse at night. My one and only boyfriend, Web, meanwhile, had been an absolute jerk who I would just as soon completely purge from my memory banks.

First and foremost, I had to figure out if Leah was even into girls. If she wasn't, then this definitely wasn't a date.

After dinner, we went for a stroll in the neighborhood. The restaurant was on McKenzie Street, which happens to be the one tiny part of our town that is in any way hip and/or funky. The college where my dad teaches is nearby, which means there are just enough people to support a small cluster of vegetarian restaurants, sleepy coffee shops, and stores selling incense and meditation chimes. The air smelled like roasting cashews, which was odd because I didn't see any street vendors.

We hadn't walked very far when we passed a comic-book shop.

"Hey!" I said. "Look, it's your almost-namesake." There was a life-size cutout of Princess Leia in the window. She was wearing the metal bikini from *The Return of the Jedi*.

"Nice," said Leah.

I grimaced. "Sorry, you're probably sick of the whole Princess Leia connection, huh?"

"A little. And it's always the metal bikini. I bet Carrie Fisher doesn't hate that metal bikini half as much as I do."

"So how come you didn't come with any friends?" I said,

changing the subject. "To do the zombie movie, I mean."

"Ah," she said. "That's complicated."

"How so?" I was certain it wasn't that she didn't have any friends. I could tell she did just from the way she talked.

"For one thing, they're not into monster movies," she said. "For me, that's a total online thing."

"What's the other thing?"

"Oh, you know. You go to a high school, you get a certain reputation, a certain circle of friends."

"Cliques," I said. "Yes, I know."

"Well, I have a clique, obviously. And they're all great people. I like them a lot. But you know how it is in high school. You can't really go out beyond your little clique. You're sort of stuck with the friends you have."

I nodded. I knew this too.

"Anyway," Leah went on, "I just decided maybe it was time to meet some new friends." She looked over at me and smiled. "And I think maybe I did."

I blushed. This is also not like me. I do not blush, literally or figuratively.

We kept walking. It was late, but there was foot traffic on the sidewalk, and the stores were all still open.

"What about you?" asked Leah.

"What about me?" I said. I wasn't sure what she was asking. Did she mean something about my friends?

"Hey," said Leah with a giggle, "you can answer the question however you want! What *about* you?"

"Well, I like my friends too," I said, thinking. "There's Gunnar. Russel, who's probably my best friend. And Russel's boyfriend, Otto."

Note my pointed use of subtext: I wanted Leah to know that there were queer people in my circle of friends. It was a very good thing Russel and Otto have gender-specific names.

We kept walking, but Leah didn't say anything. Finally, I looked over at her. She was staring at me again, smiling.

She halted suddenly. "Listen," she said. "Why don't we stop beating around the bush?"

"Huh?" I said.

"You want to know if I'm into girls," she said. "And I am. You also want to know if I'm into you. And so far, yeah, I'm into you too."

I stared at her. Subtext was definitely not Leah's thing. She said exactly what she thought, which is why she kept striking me speechless.

Subtext wasn't my thing either. I could be just as blunt as she.

"Good," I said to her. "Because so far, I'm pretty into you too."

That Monday at school, I met Russel in the hallway.

"How's it going with your parents?" I asked. His parents had recently discovered that he's gay, and things were not going well. He recounted how they had even made him go see a priest the night before.

I was dying to finally tell him all about Leah—there was no reason not to now—but the whole thing with his parents had to take precedence. There was a lot for him to talk about, and I didn't want to steal his thunder. Still, I at least wanted to come clean about my screwing up and telling Kevin about *Attack of the Soul-Sucking Brain Zombies.*

"Here's the thing," I said. "I have a confession to make. It was an accident, but I still feel really bad."

"Yeah?" said Russel. "I've got something I want to tell you too."

Before I could say anything else, however, a voice nearby said, "Did you hear? Kevin Land came out! He's *gay*!"

Russel's eyes popped open. I was pretty flabbergasted too. Suddenly everything that Kevin had been doing made perfect sense. He probably thought he was doing this really brave, impressive thing by coming out. However, the school had a gay-straight-bisexual alliance now, not to mention openly queer people like Russel and me; Kevin knew nothing that bad was going to happen to him. He'd come out exactly eight months after it might have made a difference.

The truth is, Kevin was just lonely and doing what he had to do to get Russel back. It was all a scheme. First, he'd been keeping in contact with me in order to get inside information on Russel. When I had told him about *Attack of the Soul-Sucking Brain Zombies*, he had realized it was time to strike. He had joined the cast of the movie specifically to reestablish ties with Russel. There was still the question of his being closeted, however, so now he had come out to the whole school, to finally win Russel over for good. It was all a scheme, but even I had to acknowledge that it had been expertly conceived and executed.

I felt so horrible for the part I'd played in Kevin's grand plan, even if it had been an accident.

Russel looked at me. "This doesn't change anything," he said. "Nothing at all."

"Of course not!" I said. "You're with Otto now!" Russel was smart—too smart to even *consider* going back to Kevin.

"Right," he said. "I'm with Otto." The truth, however, was that there did seem to be a note of hesitation in his voice.

I decided this wasn't a good time to tell Russel how I'd helped Kevin.

As for Leah, I decided I could tell him about that later too.

CHAPTER FOUR

I WAS DYING TO see Leah again, and I couldn't wait for the following weekend when I'd see her at the movie shoot. She'd given me her phone number, so I decided to call and just ask her out. She liked to be outspoken? Well, that happened to be my specialty. There was no way she was going to out-outspeak me.

"Hello?" she said on the other end of the phone.

"Hey," I said. "It's Min."

"Min! I was just thinking about you. What's up?"

"I just wanted to know if you wanted to go to a movie or something. Like after school on Wednesday?"

"You mean like a date?" she said, cutting right to the chase.

Leah had upped me yet again. I had truly finally met my match.

"Yes," I said, smiling into the phone. "Like a date."

"Unquestionably! Where should we meet?"

We went to a monster movie, of course. We sat in the back and held hands through the whole thing. One thing we did not do, however, was talk. Ironically, this made me like Leah even more, because I happen to detest people who talk in movies.

Afterward, we sat in the empty theater. I also like people who stay and sit through the credits. It's not so much that I care about the actual credits—though every now and then you do see something interesting. I just appreciate having a couple of minutes of quiet transition time, to slowly work my way back from the world of the movie to the "real" world. It's like after a massage, and the therapist leaves you alone in the room to gather your thoughts and get dressed again.

Finally, the credits finished rolling, so I turned to Leah and said, "Well, what did you think?"

Leah considered the question. "It had a point," she said at last. "The monster was clearly supposed to represent Marlene's unconscious fear of her father."

"So?" I asked.

"So I don't like it when monster movies have points. Monsters should be monsters, not metaphors for something else."

"I think *Attack of the Soul-Sucking Brain Zombies* has a point. I'm not sure what it is, but I think it has one."

"Yeah, I know," she said. "Something about social conformity in high school. Like *that* hasn't been done a million times before!"

"Are there any dead grandmas?" I asked.

Leah squinted at me. "Are there any what?"

"Dead grandmas. In the popcorn." I nodded to the empty bag of popcorn that we'd shared during the movie.

She kept looking at me with this absolutely blank look on her face.

"Don't you know what a dead grandma is?" I said.

"I have no idea what you're talking about," said Leah.

"Well, you know what an old maid is, right?"

"An unpopped popcorn kernel?"

"No," I said firmly. "An old maid is a half-popped popcorn kernel. A dead grandma is an unpopped popcorn kernel. I happen to love them. They're almost better than real popcorn. Crunchier."

Leah snorted. "Dead grandmas, huh? Well, that's news to me!"

"You learn something new every day. Now give me the bag. I want to see if there are any."

Leah handed me the bag. I was in luck. There were lots of them.

I slouched down in my padded seat and started gnawing on the kernels. "So," I said. "When did you come out anyway?"

"Oh," said Leah. "I haven't come out."

Suddenly I crunched down on a dead grandma that was not only unpopped but uncooked. I almost broke a tooth.

"What?" I said to Leah. "You haven't?"

She shook her head.

"But—" I started. How could this be? Leah was so confident, so outspoken. How could she not have come out?

"What?"

"I'm just really surprised no one knows you're gay. You are gay, right? Not bi?"

She stared up at the blank movie screen. "Yeah, pretty gay. And no, no one knows."

I placed the dead grandmas aside and sat upright in my chair. "Seriously?" I said. "You're not out to anyone? Not even your friends?"

"*Especially* not my friends. My parents would have an easier time of it than they would. It would just blow their little minds."

I shifted in my seat. Suddenly I realized that the floor to one side of me wasn't just sticky; it was gooey. There's a difference. I think it was someone's ketchup.

"What?" Leah asked me.

"Well, if your friends won't accept you, why are they your friends?"

Leah laughed. "It's complicated. They're good people. They're just kind of simple, most of them. They've led sheltered lives. You know, houses in the suburbs, lots of mega-churches. Most of them have never met an actual gay person."

"Well, maybe that's why you should come out. You could change their minds."

"Maybe so." Leah turned from the movie screen to me. "What is it? You seem upset."

Upset wasn't the right word. I felt like a balloon slowly leaking air. It wasn't just that I think us queer folks have a responsibility to be honest and open—to not buy into the mind-set that we have anything to be "ashamed" of, or that we have to go through the elaborate charade of pretending to be straight just to avoid "offending" someone. It was also the fact that I'd done this before—I'd been in a relationship in hiding—and it hadn't worked. At all.

"I'm just surprised," I said.

"Here's the way I see it," explained Leah. "I know who I am. I'm gay. I'm completely comfortable with that fact. I have been for a long time. But I'm also a high school student. I like my friends and my life. I like those friends and that life a lot." The worker cleaning the aisles of the theater between shows was slowly working his way closer to us, so Leah lowered her voice, which suddenly seemed so out of character. "If I come out, it'll be a really big deal, and I know for a fact a lot of my good friends won't be able to accept it. So I figure, why push it? Why not enjoy high school? Then when I get to college, people will be different. I can come out then."

"And what am I?" I said before I could stop myself. "Your little walk on the wild side?" Now I *was* upset.

Leah didn't catch the sarcasm in my voice. "Yeah!" She laughed. "Who I like isn't really anyone else's business anyway, is it?"

We both fell silent as the theater cleaner passed us by.

Leah kept looking at me. "Is this a problem?"

My head was reeling. "Well, I don't know," I admitted. "Like I said, I'm surprised. I've just never really heard of your attitude before." Even Kevin had had the good grace to at least feel *guilty* about being closeted.

"Oh. Well, do you want to go get some dinner? We can talk about it some more. I know this great place that does Korean barbecue."

I stood up. "No," I said. "I think I should be going home."

* * *

I really needed to talk to someone. Usually it was Russel I went to with problems like this, but he had so much going on with his parents that I decided I didn't want to bother him. Instead, I called Gunnar from my car and asked him if we could talk.

"Talk?" he said from his car. "About what?"

"I need your advice."

"Advice?"

"About a relationship," I said.

"And you're asking *me*?"

"Well, yes."

"Hot damn!" he said. "I'm on a roll!"

"What?" I said.

"Never mind. Look, I'm just on my way to Radio Shack. Why don't you meet me there?"

Gunnar was on his way to Radio Shack? Somehow this just figured.

Once at the store, I found him seated cross-legged on the floor in one of the back aisles. "Hi," I said.

He didn't greet me. "Did you know that over ten thousand film and video productions are released worldwide every year?" he said. "That's almost five times what it was twenty years ago. Of course that includes many TV movies, but it doesn't include TV shows."

"I didn't know that," I said. "Why exactly do you care?"

"I'm thinking of making my own movie. But it won't count as a 'release' unless I manage to sell the distribution rights."

"Ah," I said.

What was I doing? I was planning to have a heart-to-heart in the Radio Shack? This was a mistake. Gunnar just wasn't the kind of friend you talked to about girlfriend troubles. He was the kind of friend you talked to about, well, the annual number of film and video releases.

"So." He flashed me a grin. "You said you needed some advice?" Then he picked up a small box from the shelf and started reading the back.

"It's nothing," I said. "Just some girl. Look, I think I should leave you—"

"Leah?" said Gunnar.

I turned back toward him. "Wait. How did you know that? I haven't told anyone about her yet."

Gunnar had opened the box and was scrutinizing what was inside—a lens of some sort. "I could tell by the way you were talking with her on Saturday. I overheard her name later that same day." He held the lens up to his eye.

"Oh," I said. I hadn't noticed Gunnar noticing us.

"Well, yes, I'm interested in her." I explained how we'd gone out a couple of times, and we'd had a really good time, with all kinds of things in common. "But she hasn't come out," I finished. "And she has no *plans* to come out. Not until after she graduates from high school."

Gunnar looked up at me again. "Wow. After your whole thing with Terese, that must seem like a real red flag."

"Yes," I said quietly. That was it, exactly. I didn't think he'd been listening, but he was. Moreover, he'd put it all together very fast.

"Hand me that tripod," he said.

"What?" I said.

He pointed. "The long blue box. On that shelf there?"

"Oh." I handed him the box.

He opened the box and pulled out what was inside. As he was unfolding the black metal contraption, he said, "Maybe she'll change her mind."

"Who?" I said. "Leah? Oh, I really doubt it. It sounds like she's thought about this a lot."

"That is a tough one," he said thoughtfully. "What are you going to do?" I had no sense that Gunnar himself had an opinion on exactly what I should do. I think if I'd been talking to me, I would have had an opinion, a strong one. However, it was nice not to feel judged.

"Well," I said slowly. "I'm not sure. I really like her a lot. We have so much in common. And we have fun. I've never been with anyone quite like her. And she goes to a completely different school, with completely different friends. It was different with Terese, because we went to the same school, so we had to do the whole pretending thing."

"Uh-huh," said Gunnar, fiddling with the tripod but apparently still listening. "So it may not really affect you if Leah comes out or not."

"But isn't it an indication of something?" I said. "The kind of person she is? And what does it say about me? I really think people should be honest and open about who they are. Sure, there are times when a person should be circumspect, like when it comes to physical safety. But it sounds like Leah just wants to have a 'fun' high school experience."

"And you've only known her one week," he said. "If you already have questions about the kind of person she is, maybe she isn't the girl for you."

I had to acknowledge that Gunnar was pretty good at this. Maybe he didn't have a mild case of Asperger's syndrome after all. Maybe I'd just never before given him a chance to handle his own in a genuine heart-to-heart.

"I can't see her," I said. "I just can't. It contradicts everything I believe."

"Then maybe you shouldn't," said Gunnar.

"I won't," I said firmly.

"Good," he said. He turned his attention back to the tripod. "Now what say we see how that high-definition Canon camcorder up front looks atop this tripod, shall we?"

The following Saturday, we had another day of extra work on *Attack of the Soul-Sucking Brain Zombies*. The early-morning darkness was a big haze across my windshield. Once again, I arrived at the school parking lot at the same time as Kevin.

I accosted him by his car. "Kevin!" I said. "I still can't believe you're doing this."

"Doing what?" he asked.

"Stalking my best friend?"

"I told you, I'm not *stalking* him!" he said. "I just wanted to . . ." He was suddenly very twitchy.

"What?"

He shrugged. "I dunno. Keep in touch."

"Yes," I said, "I know exactly what you want to touch!"

He glared at me. "Yeah, well, did you tell him you're the one who told me about *Attack of the Soul-Sucking Brain Zombies*?"

"That is completely beside the—"

"Feeling a little guilty, huh?"

I scowled right back at him. "Look. I know I can't keep

you away from him. This is a free country—more or less. But I just want you to know that I'm on to you."

"Fine. You're on to me." He smirked at me. I'm normally a very nonviolent person, but I suddenly wanted to punch him in the face.

At that moment, however, I saw that Kevin had a black eye. I hadn't noticed it before because of the dim morning light. Somebody had already punched him in the face. Did it have something to do with his coming out?

"What?" said Kevin, a little defensively. He sensed that I'd noticed his black eye, and turned his head to one side.

"Nothing," I said, but I suddenly felt a little guilty. Had I been too hard on him? Even if his coming out was just part of a big scheme to get Russel back, and even if the school did now have openly gay kids, that didn't mean it had been easy.

I nodded to his car. "By the way. You left your headlights on."

Makeup and wardrobe turned me into a cheerleader again. They also gave my face a yellow tint, which I hoped just meant that we students had somehow started turning into zombies, and not that the makeup artist was horribly racist.

Back at the hospitality suite, I saw that Leah had also been dressed like a cheerleader. In fact, she was sitting with a couple of the other "cheerleaders" again. I didn't ignore her—I waved and sort of smiled—but I joined Russel, Gunnar, and Em, not her. I sensed Leah watching me from that other table, but she didn't come over. Clearly, she got the message I was transmitting.

A production assistant informed us they were dividing the extras into two groups.

"That'll be first and second unit," said Gunnar to Russel, Em, and me.

"What?" I said. Gunnar was back to making no sense.

He explained how half of us would be working with the director and stars, and the other half would be shooting backgrounds and exteriors with an assistant director.

I didn't care which group I ended up in—I just didn't want to be in the same one as Leah. It was awkward enough seeing her; I didn't want to have to actually *talk* to her too.

The production assistant split us into the two groups. Gunnar and I were in one group; Russel, Kevin, Em, and Leah were in the other one. I was genuinely surprised by how relieved I felt. It was almost like I was *afraid* to spend time next to Leah.

"All right!" said the production assistant. "Let's move out!"

Suddenly Russel stepped up next to me.

"Do you mind if we switch groups?" he asked.

"What?" I said. "*Why?*" This was terrible! It meant I'd have to be with Leah after all.

Russel leaned closer. "I'm trying to avoid Kevin."

I confess that at that moment, I was very, very annoyed with Russel.

"I don't think that's okay with the producers," I said. "Switching, I mean." The production assistant had said something about how important it was to stay in our groups.

Russel shook his head. "No, it's okay. I just asked."

"But—"

"What?"

I desperately tried to think of some reason to turn Russel down, but nothing came to mind. He didn't even know about Leah yet, and it was far too complicated to explain now. Besides, it was my fault that Kevin was there in the first place, so it made sense that I should be the one to make the sacrifice.

"Well, then," I said. "Okay."

"Thanks, Min," he said.

I forced out a smile and soldiered my way over to join Leah in the other group.

It's impossible to avoid someone when you've been assigned to be in the same group—but that doesn't mean I didn't try. As the production assistants led us to where we were supposed to go, I did my best to stay on the other side of the cluster of extras. Em was in my group too, also dressed like a cheerleader.

"What's up?" she asked me.

"Huh?" I said. "Oh, not much."

"I think we're turning into zombies."

"What?"

Em pointed to her face. "The yellow makeup? I think the transformation has begun."

Only now did I realize that the faces of all us teenage extras had been given a yellow tint, not just mine. I'd been too distracted before by Leah to notice.

"Oh, right," I said. "That makes sense."

A few minutes later, we reached the school gymnasium. It was an old-style gym, with dingy paint and a bruised and battered hardwood floor. It smelled like an antique shop, a mix of moisture and crusty old varnish. The camera had already been set up, and once again it looked like a typical gymnasium in front of the camera, and a hi-tech catastrophe behind it. A swarm of assistants buzzed around the director, which told me that I'd been chosen for the first unit, the one with the actual actors.

"You," said a production assistant to Leah. "Get together with the other cheerleaders."

Of course he wanted Leah to stand next to Em and me.

Leah hesitated, but I knew she had no choice but to do what the assistant had said.

"Hi," she said, not looking me in the eye.

"Hi," I said. Since she wasn't looking me in the eye, I saw no reason to keep looking *her* in the eye. In a minute, I knew they'd start rolling, so maybe I wouldn't have to talk to her after all. If this scene was like all the others, however, I knew there'd be lots of waiting around between takes.

A production assistant pointed out our "marks," which was where we extras were supposed to stand during the filming. A group of jocks in gym shorts, one of whom was Kevin, was pretending to play basketball.

"Okay," said the production assistant to us three cheerleaders. "Just act like you're practicing a cheer."

"Practicing a *cheer*?" I said dubiously.

The production assistant must have heard the note of panic in my voice, because she said, "It's okay if it looks awkward. You're turning into zombies, remember?" She demonstrated what she wanted us to do—clearly the very simplest of cheerleading moves. "Just like this," she said. "Over and over again. You can make sounds, but it'll all be rerecorded later anyway."

"Well," I said. "Okay."

"All right!" called the director, "let's try a rehearsal! Rolling! And *action!*"

Leah and I stood on our marks with Em. Pom-poms in hand, I tried to act the way the production assistant had showed us.

"No, no!" said the director. "You there!"

He was pointing right at me.

"Huh?" I said.

"Not *that* out of synch!" he said. "You're not a zombie yet!"

I buried my face in my pom-poms. "Oh, my God, I'm so bad I don't even make a good zombie-cheerleader," I moaned.

Leah heard me. "You'll be fine," she said gently. "Here, do it like this."

I looked up, and she demonstrated the cheerleader move again, very slowly.

"Wow," I said, forgetting to be uncomfortable around her. "You're good at this."

I tried my best to imitate her, and I guess I did okay, because at least the director didn't single me out for utter humiliation again.

Soon the real actors materialized on the set, and we began filming. The actors had some dialogue about their classmates, how worried they were about whatever was happening to us, zombie-wise.

There's a funny thing about acting, however: if you *act* a certain way, you start to *feel* a certain way. By acting like a cheerleader, even a part-zombie-cheerleader, I couldn't help feeling happy. Feeling happy, meanwhile, reminded me how I had felt around Leah that first night out.

After a couple of takes, the director had to talk with the actors, so we extras had some time to ourselves.

Leah stepped in close to me. Between her pom-poms and my pom-poms, it felt like we were all alone somewhere in a thicket of bushes.

"Look," she said quietly. "I've been thinking about what we talked about at that movie. About coming out? I think I sounded a little casual. Believe me, this isn't casual to me. I have thought about coming out. A lot."

"You have?" I said.

"Yeah. It's just . . . complicated. Up until now, I thought I'd made the right decision. But I can see it's bothering you, and I want you to know that I don't know what's going to be right for me a few months from now."

"Really?"

"Really," said Leah. "But for the time being, I just want to wait and see."

"That makes sense," I said. "I wouldn't want you to

come out for my sake anyway. It's got to be because you want to do it."

I hadn't been expecting Leah to bring up what we'd talked about on Wednesday. Still, I appreciated her attempt to clear the air. Moreover, what she had said really did make sense.

"Places, everyone!" called the director, interrupting us. "Let's do another take!"

That afternoon, we shot some scenes in the school hallway. First the camera just zoomed in on the door of the principal's office while we yellow-skinned extras walked awkwardly back and forth in front of it. I think it was supposed to be ominous.

Next we did the same thing to the door of the nurse's office and the janitor's storeroom.

They hadn't told us much about the actual plot of *Attack of the Soul-Sucking Brain Zombies*. Most of what I knew was what I'd been able to deduce from the scenes where I'd been in the background as an extra. It starts when a teenager named Brad moves to a new town. On the first day at his new high school, he sees all the other students clustered in tight little cliques, viciously attacking anyone new or different. On that first day, he also meets Christy, who is drop-dead gorgeous, but who the other students reject because she wears her hair in a ponytail. The point here, I'm sure, was to suggest that most of the teenagers in town were already mindless zombies of some sort. Leah may not have liked that the movie had a point, but at least it was one that I could wholeheartedly agree with.

As the days go by, Brad and Christy quickly discern that the other students in their school are turning more zombielike every day—stumbling around stiffly, becoming decreasingly verbal. It's almost as if something is sucking out their very souls. The question is, who is sucking the souls out, how, and why? The suspects are apparently the fat, bald principal, the buxom *Playboy*-centerfold-turned-school-nurse, and the macho school janitor.

Despite knowing all this, however, I was no closer to learning what a "brain zombie" is.

"Hey," said Leah to me between takes, "you want to get dinner again tonight after the shoot?"

"Dinner?" I said.

"Yeah, we can talk some more about, well, what we were talking about before. Besides, you owe me."

I narrowed my eyes. "For what?"

"For teaching you how to not look like an idiot with the pom-poms!"

I couldn't deny it. The truth is, I felt much better about

Leah now. It was what she had said before, about how meeting me had started her pondering about coming out.

"Okay," I said. "Let's get some dinner."

Here's the thing. If Russel hadn't wanted to switch units with me, I might not have been forced to talk to Leah, and we might not have made up. As I was thinking about this, I realized that the first time we'd talked was also because of Russel—because he'd gotten his plastic number mixed up with mine.

In short, I had him to thank for this new relationship of mine, and he didn't even know it.

69

CHAPTER FIVE

We went back to that Ethiopian restaurant on McKenzie Street. We had said we were going to talk more about her decision to come out, or not, but it didn't come up. I guess we both concluded that, for the time being, there wasn't anything more to be said.

Dinner was good, but not like it was the first time around. It's possible that what was different wasn't the restaurant, but Leah, or at least the fact that my feelings toward her were a little more wary now.

After dinner, we decided to meander along McKenzie Street again. Thanksgiving was the following Thursday, and the street and the shops that lined the sidewalk had now been decorated for Christmas. So much had changed in just a week; it was like a completely different street. Fairy lights twinkled in the bare branches of the trees along the sidewalk, and the air smelled of peppermint hot chocolate and wet cardboard. Everywhere we looked, stars glittered, mangers glowed, and in the windows of all the shops, distorted reflections of Leah and me undulated on the surface of a hundred colored Christmas balls.

"So," said Leah. "The movie. Who do you think is turning the school into zombies? The principal, the nurse, or the janitor?"

"That's a good question," I said. "I think it's the nurse. There's like three female speaking roles in the whole movie, so it would just figure that one of them turns out to be the villain. It's either the nurse, or someone completely off the radar. One of the other students maybe? The captain of the football team?"

"I think it's the janitor," said Leah.

"Really? No. That's too obvious. It's *always* the janitor. That's a cliché."

"Maybe so, but I still think it's him."

"I think you're wrong."

We walked on in silence. Somewhere in the distance, a Christmas ornament shattered. Was all this a sign? Was something about Leah and me fundamentally wrong?

We passed the shop with the cardboard cutout of

Princess Leia in the metal bikini. A lot had changed since last week, but not everything.

Leah stopped suddenly.

"What?" I said.

She had spied something farther down the sidewalk. "Nothing," she said. "Just some friends of mine. From school."

"Really? Let's say hi." The truth is, I was exceedingly curious about these "friends" of hers.

"Oh." Leah shrugged. "I don't know."

"What? Ashamed of me?"

"No!" said Leah. I had meant it as a joke, but Leah had responded so quickly I wondered if maybe she really *was* ashamed of me. "I mean," she went on, "you can meet them if you want."

"Okay."

Leah treaded lightly down that sidewalk, as if she were walking on crossbeams in the attic and was worried that she might step through the ceiling.

I didn't see her friends anywhere. The only other high school students on McKenzie Street right then were three cheerleaders on the corner. They had donned jackets, with sweatpants under their skirts, as if they'd been outside for a while. They'd transformed a plastic garbage can into a big, hollow papier-mâché turkey and were using it to solicit donations for a local food bank.

I turned to Leah. "Wait. *Those* aren't your friends, are they?"

Right then, one of the cheerleaders-in-sweats noticed us.

"Leah?" she said. "Is that *you?*"

"Yeah," said Leah. "Hi, Dade, hi, Savannah, hi, Alexis."

We walked the rest of the way to the corner. Having been on the movie set all day, I was used to seeing people dressed up like cheerleaders. These three, however, weren't just dressed like cheerleaders; they really *were* cheerleaders. The differences were subtle but profound. Diamond stud earrings, for example—practical given all the jumping required, but clearly expensive. The hair was different too: styled, not cut; swept, not curled.

"What is that you're *wearing?*" one of the other girls—Savannah—said to Leah. She meant the navy Union jacket with the epaulets, which Leah had on again today.

"This?" said Leah. "I just thought it looked fun. Dade, Alexis, Savannah," she quickly went on, "this is Min. She's one of the extras from that movie I was telling you about."

"Oh," said Dade, blinking at me. "Hi."

"Nice to meet you," said Savannah.

"Great turkey," I said. "Really clever."

I couldn't help but think that Leah's friends were staring at my purple hair. Or maybe it was the fact that I'm Asian. I wasn't sure what they were looking at, but I definitely had that on-display feeling. I also detected a foul smell wafting over us from somewhere nearby—a tipped garbage can maybe.

"So," said Leah. "What are you guys up to?"

Dade sighed. "What does it look like? It's *so* not fair. Crystal, Cyndee, and Veronica got to go to the mall—this part of town totally gives me the creeps. And what is with that *smell*? I think there's a dead body in that alley back there!"

Alexis leaned toward Leah and me. "Total college boy-babe at twelve o'clock."

Leah made a perfunctory glance over her shoulder. "Oh, yeah, very cute. Listen," she said to her friends. "Min has to get home, so I'll see you around, okay?"

"Okay," said Savannah. "Bye!"

"Bye, Min!" said Dade. She made the "phone" sign with her thumb and little finger and waggled in the general vicinity of her ear. "Leah, *call me!*"

"Cheerleaders?" I said to Leah a few minutes later, once we'd left her friends back around the corner. "Your friends are *cheerleaders*?"

"What?" said Leah defensively. "What's wrong with cheerleaders?"

"Do you really have to ask?"

"That's just pure prejudice, you know that? You're just relying on stereotypes."

"Is that right?" I said. " 'Crystal, Cyndee, and Veronica got to go to the mall—this part of town totally gives me the creeps'! 'Total college boy-babe at twelve o'clock'!"

Leah held up her hands. "Okay, okay! They're stupid and superficial! I told you that already, remember?"

"You did, but what you didn't say is *why* they're your friends!"

"They just are, okay? Why is that any of your business? I've known them a long time. They've got good qualities too, you know."

"And what was that they were saying about your clothes?"

Leah tried to shrug it off. "This just isn't what I usually wear, okay?"

"Well, what do you usually—" Suddenly, however, I knew the answer. "Oh my God! You're a cheerleader too! Aren't you? That's why you made such a good cheerleader back at the shoot. Because you *are* one!" Why hadn't this occurred to me before?

This made Leah angry. "No!" she said. "I'm not! I told you I wasn't, and I don't appreciate your accusing me of lying. I was a cheerleader in the seventh grade. But I hurt my knee, and I had to drop out."

"You hurt your knee? You didn't mention that before!"

"What difference does *that* make?"

"The difference," I said like I was hurling a thunderbolt, "is that if you hadn't injured your knee, I bet you'd *still* be a cheerleader!"

"Maybe! So what? How is that a lie?"

"It's like you changed everything about yourself!" I gestured at her. "Like this is all an act."

"I *did* change everything!" said Leah, exasperated. "Because I wanted to meet some new friends! I told you that too. Yeah, maybe I even wanted to find a girlfriend. So yeah, I changed my hair a little, took off some of my makeup, and got some new clothes. So? That was the whole point. I wanted to meet *new* friends. *Different* friends. If I'd dressed the way I usually dress, I just would have ended up with the same old friends!"

I turned away. "It just seems . . . dishonest." Like everything about her, I thought. I acknowledge, however, that technically she hadn't lied about any of this.

Leah faced me and took my hands in hers, even though her friends were still just one block over. "Look," she said. "I'm sure this must be very weird for you. But that person that I am when I'm with my other friends? That's the act. The person I am with you? This is the real me."

I looked up at her. "Really?"

"Really."

I tried to take all this in. "Okay. I'm sorry I overreacted."

"It's okay," she said with a smile. I couldn't help but notice, however, that the second I had apologized, she released both my hands.

That Monday during after-school tea with my mother, I filled her in on everything that had happened with Leah so far.

"That's not good," said my mom, unwrapping her Ding Dong.

If you had told me six months earlier that I'd be sitting having tea with my mother taking about girl problems, I would *not* have believed you. However, had you told me that she'd be wearing a horrible denim jumpsuit at the time, which she was, that I definitely would have believed.

"So what do I do?" I asked. "I really like her. But those friends of hers! They're terrible. I can't imagine what she sees in them."

"You're not dating her friends," said my mom. "You're dating her."

"But they *are* her friends! They make me question what

I see in Leah. First, it was her attitude about coming out. Now this."

My mom sipped her tea. Her placid demeanor was beyond annoying. When she wanted to, she could still play the quiet Chinese wife.

"*What?*" I asked. "You can say what you really think."

"My mother used to tell me this little story," said my mom. "It's a fable. There was a priest who lived in a cave in the mountains above a village. He was a very virtuous man, and when he came to town to teach, the whole village would stop and listen to him. In exchange for the wisdom of his teachings, the villages would give him the food and other things he needed to live."

"Wait," I said. "You're actually telling me a fable to make a point? Do people really *do* that?"

"Just hush," said my mom. "Anyway, the priest liked that the village thought so highly of him. He thought very highly of himself, for he knew that he was the wisest, most virtuous person in the whole countryside."

"And how exactly does this story relate to me?" I said. "You think I'm sanctimonious?"

"A little," said my mom.

"*What?*" I said, but it was mostly false outrage. Like me, my mom could be pretty blunt, but that was part of what I liked about her.

"You're not hushing. Just eat your Ding Dong and listen, okay? Anyway, one day the priest thought, Why should I travel all the way down to the village to teach? I am the one with the wisdom. The villagers should be the ones to come up *here*. And so he waited. Down in the village, the villagers wondered what had happened to the priest. They hiked up to his cave, where the priest explained that if they still wanted to hear his teachings, from now on they would have to come to him."

"Did they come?" I asked. I was still offended that my mom had called me sanctimonious, but I was intrigued by the story.

My mom nodded. "They did indeed. The priest would have the villagers gather in a big cavern in the middle of his cave, and he would teach. And did he teach! He dazzled them with his great wisdom. It got so he never even needed to leave his cave at all."

"But?" I said.

"But what?" said my mom, taking a bite of her own Ding Dong.

"Oh, please. He was a jerk to the villagers. These things always have a way of backfiring."

My mom smiled. "Well, one day he woke, and it seemed as if his body had magically grown bigger overnight. At first he thought it was all in his imagination. But the next day, he had grown bigger still. After a few days, even the villagers started to notice it. When they asked him about his sudden growth, he said, 'Well, as you all know, I am so much wiser and more pure than most people. And now that my soul has grown so big, my body had no choice but to grow bigger too, to keep up with it!'"

"Uh-huh," I said. "What did I say? Karmic revenge."

"As the days and weeks went by, the priest kept growing larger still, until he was a giant. Which is only fitting! thought the priest. I have always been a giant among men. Now I am an *actual* giant! In all this time, however, the priest had not left the cave. But one day he decided he wanted to see the sunrise over the mountains. And when he went to leave the cave—"

"He found he had grown too large to get out," I said.

"Exactly," said my mother. "Well, the priest thought, so I can't leave the cave. The villagers will still come to me, to hear my great wisdom! But then one day, a new teacher came to the village, one who had new teachings, things they had not heard before. Soon the fickle villagers had forgotten all about the priest in the cave."

"Leaving him trapped inside," I finished.

My mom nodded again. "To subsist on rainwater and rats and spiders."

I sat upright in my chair. "So I'm trapped in a cave? Is that what you're saying? I'm just that sanctimonious?"

"Min—"

"So, what, I should just ignore my principles? Not be bothered by Leah's brainless friends, or the fact that she's lying to the world?"

My mom shook her head. "That's not what the story is saying at all."

"Then what *is* it saying?"

"Just that if you demand that the whole world lives on your terms—that if you require that everyone sees everything *your* way—well, you can end up in a place that's awfully small."

I hesitated. I was still a little annoyed. I had to concede, however, that my mom's story made a legitimate point.

CHAPTER SIX

RUSSEL'S BOYFRIEND, OTTO, LIVED in another state, but he was coming to visit over Thanksgiving break. Wednesday night, Russel, Gunnar, Em, and I went to pick him up at the airport.

In the car on the ride over, I wanted to confess to Russel everything that was going on with Leah. I'd already told Gunnar, who had probably told Em. Things were still rough for Russel with his parents, but he wasn't in crisis mode anymore. He was my best friend, and he deserved to know.

For some reason, however, I couldn't get the words out. I thought about all the times I had acted all holier-than-thou around Russel. The year before, we'd started this secret gay-straight alliance called the Geography Club. At one point, we'd had to decide whether to stand up for this kid who everyone thought was gay and who everyone was bullying, or to stay quiet and protect ourselves from maybe being bullied too. This was the time that Kevin had acted like such a baby. I, of course, had made a big stink about how we couldn't compromise our principles. Yet now here I was with Leah, this person who basically agreed with Kevin, that gay people should just stay silent if it means jeopardizing their popularity. It wasn't that Russel would judge me for being with her; he wasn't like that. Still, having to explain it to him would make me feel like a hypocrite. Maybe I *was* a hypocrite. Or maybe my mom was right when she'd implied that I could be sanctimonious.

"So," said Russel as we drove along. "Has anyone figured out what the hell a 'brain zombie' is yet?"

"That is a damn good question!" said Em. "What *is* a brain zombie?"

"They haven't mentioned it in any of the scenes I've been in," I said.

"Me neither," said Russel.

"Just because we don't know the explanation," said Gunnar, "that doesn't mean there *isn't* one. Or maybe it's just a *working* title." Even now, he took any disparagement of the movie as a personal criticism.

"Okay," said Russel. "So I have another question."

"What's that?" said Em.

"Who do we think is turning the school into zombies? The principal, the janitor, or the school nurse?" By now, everyone else had figured out as much of the plot as I had.

"The school nurse?" said Em. "You mean Nurse Busty?"

"She's not that bad," said Gunnar.

"You would say that!" said Em wryly.

"What?" he said cluelessly. "No, wait, I'm not attracted to big boobs."

She whacked him on the arm. "Thanks! Thanks a lot!"

"It's probably the janitor," said Russel.

This made me perk up. Russel thought the villain was the janitor?

"I think so too," said Em.

"Yeah," said Gunnar. "I totally think it's the janitor."

"Wait," I said, surprised. "You guys all think it's the janitor?" How was this possible? Russel, Gunnar, and Em were all supposed to be *smart*!

They all nodded or shrugged.

"There is no *way* it's the janitor," I said. "It's either the nurse, or someone completely different—maybe the captain of the football team."

"Min," said Russel. "In a nutshell? You're nuts."

"I am not!"

"Sorry, Min," said Em, "but Russel's right. It's the janitor."

"But what about the fact that the nurse is giving them all flu shots?" I said. "*That's* how she's turning the students into zombies!"

"It's a red herring," said Russel. "There's a reason they have the janitor acting all macho."

"That's the red herring!" I exclaimed. "It can't be the janitor. It's *always* the janitor!" Telling Russel about Leah could wait. For the time being, I had to convince him and the others that it was Nurse Busty who was turning the students of our new high school into monsters—"brain zombies" or otherwise.

The next day, Thanksgiving, I had an early dinner with my family. My mom wore a sweater with a turkey on it that simply had to be seen to be believed. Afterward, I drove over to Gunnar's, where he, Em, Russel, and Otto were having a little Thanksgiving dinner of their own. Once again, I was somewhat preoccupied by the whole situation with Leah, but I confess, I had a very nice time.

At one point, I excused myself to go use the bathroom. The door opened, and the smell of cheap potpourri wafted out from inside. I'm not a big fan of potpourri, even the expensive stuff, but when it comes to bathrooms, I guess it's better than the alternative.

Otto stepped out.

"Oh," I said. "Hey."

"Hey, Min!" he said.

Otto was a friend of mine from summer camp, but I hadn't spent any time alone with him since he'd arrived the day before.

"It's so great you came to visit," I said. "Russel's really excited."

"You think?"

I was surprised he said this. Then again, Russel *had* been a little distracted at dinner. Was something going on between them?

"He is," I said. "Trust me."

Otto leaned back against the wall in the hallway. "I was so pissed when Russel's parents found out about me. I thought I'd have to cancel." Russel's parents had refused to let Otto stay with them, so he'd ended up staying with Gunnar.

"Are you excited about the movie shoot tomorrow?" I asked. Russel had arranged for Otto to be an extra too.

Otto thought for a second. "Yeah," he said. "Part of me

wishes Russel and I could be alone. But I know Russel really wants to do it. Are you having fun?"

"On the movie?"

He nodded.

Was I having fun on the movie? I honestly didn't know. The past few weeks had all been about Leah. I had barely paid any attention to everything else going on around me.

"Sure," I said. "I guess so."

"What?"

I sighed. "Well, it's complicated."

"Too complicated to talk about just passing someone in a hallway, huh?"

I laughed. "Yes, I think so."

"Yeah," he said. "I know what you mean." He thought for a second. "But I have an idea."

"Yes?"

"Let's give each other some advice."

"Advice? What kind of advice?"

"Just . . . advice."

"But we don't even know each other's problems," I protested.

He winked at me. "That's why this is such a great idea."

"Okay. But you have to go first."

He thought again, then said, "'Before you run in double harness, look well to the other horse.'"

"What?" I said, laughing out loud. "Where did that come from!"

"I don't know," said Otto, smiling. "I just always liked the way it sounded. Besides, it's good advice."

"I guess it is—if you live in a Charles Dickens novel."

Otto kept smiling. "Well?"

"Well what?" I said.

"Does it help you with your problem?"

I had to think about it. Here's the thing. It fit the situation with Leah perfectly.

I stopped laughing. "Yes, actually. What do you know about that?"

"So?" he said. "What's your advice for me?"

It was a little discombobulating how comfortable I felt talking to Otto. It immediately reminded me of being with Russel. I recalled how at camp I'd felt that way around Otto too; the two of them were so much alike that being with one was almost like being with the other. They were both sensitive and funny and so very clever. They were also emotional and passionate, but still very much optimistic about life. Mostly, though, they were both just fun to be around.

"Give Russel a break," I said at last. "I don't know why he's been distracted, but don't worry. He really, really loves you. And God, is he the right guy for you."

"Wait," he said, laughing. "That doesn't count. That's real advice!"

"I know," I said, turning for the bathroom. "But I still think it's good."

I was dreading the next day, Friday, when we'd go back to shooting the movie. I'd seen Leah on the set the previous Sunday, but we had barely talked since Saturday night when we'd run into her friends on McKenzie Street. I had no idea what I was going to say to her, or if I should even say anything.

Friday was the day they finally turned us into full-fledged zombies. They made me up as a zombie-cheerleader, with rotting green skin and bloodstained pom-poms. As zombies go, I looked amazing, but I couldn't enjoy it, because I was preoccupied with Leah.

I was the last person out of makeup, so when I finally got to the set, they had already finished shooting the first scene. The second shot of the day was another view of the hallway outside the principal's office. When I got there, I saw that they had made Leah up as a zombie-band geek.

They'd even given her a bent flute.

This was ironic. I was the cheerleader, and she was the geek. It also meant that if they did things the way they always had before, they would cluster us together with the other members of our cliques: cheerleader with cheerleader, band geek with band geek. In other words, I wouldn't have to spend the whole day standing next to her. In *other* other words, I was avoiding her again. With all the avoiding that I'd been doing lately, I felt like I was back in the seventh grade.

Careful not to make eye contact with Leah, I joined Russel, Otto, Em, and Gunnar.

The director explained how we extras were just supposed to trudge back and forth in front of the door to the principal's office. This time, however, a puddle of blood slowly seeps out from the crack under the entrance. The students at the school, full-fledged zombies now, take no notice of it, and slog right across the growing pool, smearing bloody streaks and planting red footsteps up and down the hall.

Clearly something horrible had happened behind that door. Had the principal killed someone, proving that it was he who was responsible for turning the school into zombies? Or perhaps some zombie had killed the principal, eliminating him as a suspect completely. As extras, we weren't privy to the scene behind the door. Any screams, meanwhile, would be added later, in looping, so I had no way of knowing whose blood was on the floor.

We did the first take. I passed right by Leah, but we were both in zombie mode, so I didn't have to acknowledge her. The fake blood on the floor smelled oddly sweet, like the frosting on a birthday cake.

"Excellent!" said the director when we were done. "Now let's do it again!"

Doing another take, however, meant cleaning up the mess we'd made on the floor—not to mention replacing all of our now-bloody shoes. Something told me we weren't going to be doing fifteen takes of this particular scene.

While production assistants mopped up all the blood, other assistants gave each of us a box of new tennis shoes. Leah was already changing her shoes at one end of a row of folding chairs. I sat down next to Russel at the opposite end of the row.

"So this either proves it's the principal, or it eliminates him completely," I said to him.

"What?" he said. "Min, there's no way it's the principal. I already told you, it's the janitor."

"Personally, I still think it's the nurse," I said. "Or the

captain of the football team."

Russel laughed. "It's the janitor! Trust me, Min. There's a reason why we shot that scene in the computer lab."

"It's not the janitor!" I expostulated. "What about whatever's locked in the nurse's closet?"

"Your skin is coming unglued," said Russel.

"What?" Was this some kind of new insult?

"Seriously," he said. "Your peeling zombie skin? It's peeling all the way off."

I reached up to feel my face. He was right. I was losing one of the little patches of green skin that they'd glued to my face to make it look like I was rotting.

"I'd go to makeup and have them reattach it," said Russel. He nodded toward the still-messy floor. "You've got plenty of time. They're not done cleaning."

"Okay," I said. "But this isn't over. When I get back, we're going to have this out once and for all."

Russel rolled his eyes. I stood up and proceeded toward the makeup department.

I turned a corner and immediately found myself face to face with Leah. I thought she'd still be back changing her shoes, but she must have gone to the bathroom.

"Uh, hi," she said.

"Oh," I said. "Hi."

She fidgeted, looking as edgy as I felt. Why had I listened to Russel about going to makeup? He'd managed to get me mixed up with Leah yet *again*. This time, however, I didn't want to have anything to do with her.

"Just so I'm clear," said Leah. "You're avoiding me, right?"

"Yes," I admitted.

"Oh. Well, thanks for being honest."

"It's not you," I said. "It's me." I thought about what I'd just said. "Wait, that sounds like I'm breaking up with you."

"Breaking up?" said Leah. "I didn't even know we were going out."

I smiled. "You haven't been a lesbian very long, have you? You're never supposed to know when you're going out with someone."

"Wouldn't you *have* to know?" she said. "Wouldn't there be, like, kissing? Candlelight dinners and sweet nothings whispered in the ear?"

"Like I said, you *really* haven't been a lesbian very long!"

At that, she laughed. The lightened mood made me laugh too.

"Anyway," I went on, "I *am* avoiding you, but it's not because I don't want to see you."

"Um," said Leah, confused. "Okay."

I shook my head. "I had no idea this would be so complicated." I tried again. "I do want to keep seeing you. I just wanted to think about what we've talked about. Get a sense of how I feel about everything. I didn't know what to say to you—as you can kind of tell from this conversation right now, I might add. Anyway, that's why I was avoiding you."

"Ah," she said. "That makes sense. Well, now that the avoiding-me thing is shot to hell, any chance you want to come over to my house to watch DVDs after the shoot?"

"Unquestionably," I said.

94   Leah's bedroom wasn't what I was expecting at all.

She had framed movie posters on the walls, from monster flicks like *Dr. Jekyll and Mr. Hyde* and *Cat People*. She also had one of Princess Leia from the original *Star Wars*, but not in a metal bikini. She had shelves and shelves of books—almost all science fiction and fantasy. She had good taste too: excellent books by Jacqueline Carey, Octavia Butler, and George R. R. Martin; graphic novels from Neil Gaiman and Alan Moore; and bound reprintings of old EC and DC Comics.

For knickknacks, she had dragons and plastic figurines of classic monsters like Wolfman and Frankenstein. Not a pony or Barbie anywhere in sight.

Her room was dark, but not drab; clean, but not neat-freaky; and quirky, but not cluttered. It smelled like lavender—real lavender—but I couldn't find the source. The bed had been made, but only very loosely.

In short, it was the bedroom of someone who, if I didn't know her, I would really *want* to know. That made me think that she hadn't been lying when she'd said that the Leah I knew was the "real" one, not the girl who hung out with her cheerleader friends.

By now she had closed the door to her bedroom. On the back, there was a big poster of Xena and Gabrielle from the TV series *Xena: Warrior Princess*.

"Oh, my God!" I said. "You *are* a lesbian!"

"You weren't sure?" said Leah. "And you can tell that from my *Xena* poster?"

I gave her the fish-eye. "You're kidding, right?"

She laughed. "I love that show. I have all six seasons. And it's not just the lesbian subtext or whatever. I like that it's so dark—that the world is this bleak, scary place, and that Xena has this ugly, evil past that she has to atone for."

"Oh, I *completely* agree," I said. "And I just *love* all the self-sacrifice. Again and again, Xena has to make some impossible sacrifice—giving her son away to be raised by centaurs, taking Callisto's place in hell, even forfeiting her life!—all because she has to make amends for that evil past, but also because these things are just the right thing to do. And most of the time, no one except her sidekick Gabrielle even knows the true cost of her sacrifice. I *love* that!"

Leah laughed again.

I looked at Leah's coat, which she'd put on her bed.

"Hey," I said, "let's switch coats."

"What?" she said.

"Let's trade."

"I'm, like, three feet taller than you."

"Okay, then let me just try it on." I slipped hers on. It was way too big, even with the sleeves rolled up. However, it smelled like her. It felt like I was wrapping her around me. "Just for a little while, okay?"

"Really?" said Leah. "Like I'm a guy giving you his letterman jacket?"

"Yes, except that I don't go for the butch-femme thing. And even if I did, you would so not be the butch."

"Okay. It's not like I can wear that jacket to school anyway."

I fingered one of the epaulets. "What do you want to do now?"

Suddenly there was a knock on the door. "Leah!" her

mom called. "Your friends are here!"

Leah and I stared at each other, eyes wide. Friends? Outside the door, the stairs squeaked and groaned under approaching footsteps.

A second later, Dade, Savannah, and Alexis glided into the room. Each one was wearing torn jeans and sipping a different brand of diet cola.

"Hey, Leah!" said Dade.

"Oh," said Alexis, noticing me. "Min." She wasn't being an outright bitch, but she didn't sound ecstatic to see me.

"Hi," I said to them all. Suddenly the bedroom felt too crowded, like an elevator way over capacity. I definitely wanted to get off.

They all took seats—on the bed and at the desk. They reminded me of cats, sinking into sleek, angular resting positions. Leah and I stayed standing. If we'd been animals, it would have been something twitchy and anxious, like squirrels.

"So what's going on?" Leah asked her friends.

"Nada," said Savannah. "We were just hanging." She looked at me. "What, did you and Leah trade jackets?"

"I'm just borrowing it," I said. I could tell from her expression exactly what she thought of that decision.

"We were just hanging too," said Leah. As I watched, she relaxed before my eyes, becoming more catlike by the second. I tried to relax like Leah, but the best I could do was only something slightly less twitchy, like a rabbit. How was it, I wondered, that her friends couldn't see from her bedroom what a dyke Leah was? She had a poster of Xena on her door, for Christ's sake! Was it because she didn't "look" like a lesbian?

"I can't *believe* Debbie didn't go crazy when he posted those pictures on the Internet!" Savannah was saying.

"Don't tell me she didn't know," said Alexis. "She knew. I know she knew."

"Why didn't she post the pictures of Zack?" said Dade. "Damn, he is so hot."

"Yeah," said Alexis, "but that army surplus thing has so got to go."

"I like it," said Savannah. "It goes with his Hummer."

Leah's friends kept talking about their school and people they knew. No one asked me anything, and Leah hardly contributed anything herself. I pretended to listen, but really I tuned them out. At this point, my plan was to stay as long as necessary to be polite, and then take the first opportunity to leave.

"Oh, my God, Hunter is such a fag!" said Dade suddenly.

That perked me up.

"Did you see that shirt?" Dade went on. "He looked like a pirate!"

"A *gay* pirate!" said Savannah.

"A gay pirate from the sixties," said Alexis. "It was tie-dyed, people. *Tie-dyed!*"

"And don't get me started on all his little friends," added Dade. "I see them prancing down the hallways on their way to play rehearsal."

Leah didn't say anything. Suddenly it was absolutely imperative that she rearrange the plastic monsters on one of her shelves. That said, at least she didn't look like a relaxed cat anymore.

"Why do they have to go to our school anyway?" said Savannah. "I thought they had their own high school. Harvey Mink or something."

"Milk," said Dade. "And that's in New York."

"So?" said Savannah. "Why can't they go there? We can ship all the fags to New York, then we can blow up the bridges, like what they did to all the criminals in that movie *Escape from New York*."

I glared at Leah, but she was snapping a tiny plastic bat back onto Dracula's shoulder, so she didn't notice. Meanwhile, her friends didn't notice my bug-eyed expression either, because they were still ignoring me, as if I didn't even exist.

Leah had to know I was upset by her friends' rank homophobia. How could *she* not be upset? So why didn't she *say* something? However, no matter how hard I glared at her, she wouldn't even look up.

CHAPTER SEVEN

HERE'S THE THING. I wasn't that upset with Leah's friends for making those antigay comments. Yes, they were stupid and bigoted, but that was about what I expected from people like them.

What upset me was that Leah didn't say anything—that she *still* wasn't saying anything.

My eyes were lasers burning into her head. She fiddled with her mummy now, which was ironic, because in my mind she'd turned into something of a monster herself.

At last she turned to face her friends.

"Did you guys know there's no evidence that pirates ever made anyone walk the plank?" she said loudly. "Which isn't to say they didn't throw a lot of people overboard."

Nice try, I thought. Changing the subject, however, is the same as not saying anything.

"Uh, that's real interesting," said Alexis. "But what the hell does that have to do with anything?"

"Nothing," said Leah. "You guys just mentioned pirates."

"*Gay* pirates!" said Savannah. "We were talking about Hunter and his faggy friends."

I still didn't speak up, even though it was killing me not to. I had to see if Leah ever would. It was a test of sorts.

"Well," said Leah, trying again to change the subject, "he doesn't have anything on Loren. The guy has, what, one T-shirt?"

"Someone told me it's not all the same shirt," said Dade. "He has, like, ten identical ones."

"That's true!" said Savannah. "He sits in front of me in English, and there's this yellow stain on the neck. But it only shows up once every two weeks!"

In other words, this time it worked, and the subject really did change. Leah never had said anything about the antigay comments.

Dade and the others kept chattering on about boys, and clothes, and TV shows. By the time they rose to leave twenty minutes later, no one had even noticed that in all the time since they'd made those homophobic comments, I still hadn't said one word.

"Okay," said Leah as they were leaving. "Bye! See you soon."

They left, and Leah and I were alone.

I cleared my throat.

"Don't start," said Leah.

"Don't start what?" I said. I didn't sound nearly as innocent as I'd intended.

"Look, you didn't say anything either."

This made me mad. "Because I was waiting to see if you would! Because I thought you would jump all over me if I did!"

She fell straight back on her bed. "Min," she said wearily, "I already told you. I'm not ready to come out."

"This has nothing to do with coming out!" I shouted. We had officially reached the outburst stage. "This has to do with not tolerating bigotry!"

"Yeah, well, in this case, it's the same thing."

"Let me get this straight. If you'd called them on those stupid jokes, they would have thought you were a lesbian?"

"Maybe! Between that and finding me alone in my room with you."

"The girl with purple hair."

"Yes! The girl with purple hair! I keep explaining this to you, and you say you understand, but you never do!"

I fumbled for the door. "I can't talk about this right now. I need to think."

"Fine," said Leah. "Go *think*. While you're gone, I'll think too!"

I slammed her door on the way out.

I had already left the house and was in my car before I realized that I was still wearing her coat.

I was too mad to think; it was all I could do to keep my hands on the wheel as I drove home.

A few minutes after setting out, however, I passed a familiar car. I was sure it was Kevin's. I don't know why I cared, but I couldn't help but wonder where he was going on a Friday night.

I was still too furious with Leah to think about the whole situation with her. Kevin's car, however, suddenly gave me something else to focus on. I clung to it like a boulder in the middle of a raging current.

I needed direction, and Kevin's car gave me some, so I turned my car around and followed his.

He pulled into the lot of a deserted park. A playground of sand abutted a soccer field. Beyond the playground, next to a greenbelt, a picnic gazebo rose from a strip of grass.

I parked my car on a side street and watched as Kevin hurried across the park toward the gazebo. I recognized this place. It's where Russel and Kevin used to meet when they were still going out. Russel had pointed it out to me.

That had to be why Kevin had come here now: to rendezvous with Russel. They must have made plans to meet just like before.

Were they getting back together again? Suddenly I understood why Russel had been so distracted lately. But what about Otto? Was Russel planning on leaving him?

I thought about the conversation I'd had with Otto the day before, how he had reminded me so much of Russel. Otto and Russel were perfect together. Kevin, meanwhile, was a selfish weasel.

There wasn't anyone waiting for Kevin under the picnic gazebo. He had beat Russel here.

I desperately needed to talk to Kevin before Russel arrived. I slipped out of my car and started toward the gazebo. I passed the playground of sand, which had a jungle gym made up of two sets of a monkey bars—one in the shape of a teepee, one in the shape of a wagon. The sun had set long ago, and the park had no streetlamps, so everything was dark. I was struck by how different everything looked at night. Nothing had texture or shade; everything was either light or dark. It felt like I'd stepped right into a black-and-white movie. I could only hope it wasn't a monster movie.

As I approached the gazebo, Kevin peered out at me through the darkness. "Russel?" he said. "Is that you?" He had mistaken me for a guy because I was wearing Leah's coat.

"No," I said, stepping into the gazebo. Russel hadn't been kidding about this place being stinky. The smell of methane was overpowering.

"*Min?*" he said, flabbergasted. "What are you doing here?"

"The question is, what are *you* doing here?"

He turned away. "That's none of your business." In the black-and-white movie in my mind, he looked different too: flatter, almost two-dimensional, but cleaner. His features stood out in the moonlight, a classic leading man.

"Come on," I said. "I know why you're here. You're meeting Russel."

The silhouette that was Kevin just shrugged. "Maybe."

"Please don't do this."

"Don't do what?" said Kevin.

"What you've been doing all along, which is try to win him back."

"I don't see how any of this is any of your busi—"

"He's my best friend," I spoke emphatically. "I care about him. That makes it my business."

"Min, just go."

I couldn't go yet. It had something to do with what had just happened with Leah. I couldn't figure out how to react to her, what was the right thing to do. It was all blurry in my mind. This situation was clearer. I guess I had more perspective when it came to someone else's life.

"Russel has moved on," I said. "He has a new boyfriend now. It's time for you to let him go."

"I'm sorry," said Kevin. "But don't you think that's Russel's decision, not yours?"

"You're right," I said. "It's not my decision. But it's not Russel's either. It's yours."

Kevin looked over at me, squinting. The confusion was clear on his face.

"I'm sure Russel still has feelings for you," I said. "Don't you know how you broke his heart? He pretended to be strong, but he wasn't. He was devastated. Do you know how many times he cried in my arms? His feelings were so strong then that he just might go and do something really stupid now and dump Otto to get back together with you. And why wouldn't he? You've planned and schemed it all perfectly. Don't think I don't know how you left your headlights on on purpose!"

"It wasn't a scheme," mumbled Kevin.

"Is it because you're an athlete? You like to win? It somehow drives you crazy that you lost Russel, so now you want him back? That's it, isn't it?"

"No!" said Kevin, his fists clenched, wrestling with imaginary manacles and chains. "That's *not* it! Did you ever think that maybe I love him too? That maybe I cried just as much as he did? And that eventually I realized what a stupid mistake I'd made? You think it was easy coming out to the whole school? When you guys came out, you had each other, the whole Geography Club. But I had to do it alone! But I did it for him, because I know how important it is to him."

108   Kevin had a point. It hadn't occurred to me that he'd had to come out alone. He'd probably also lost friends, and quite a bit of his popularity, because of his action. I remembered his black eye that one morning in the parking lot. I couldn't help but think of Leah. Would she pay such a price to get together with me? The evidence spoke against it.

"I'm sorry," I whispered to Kevin. "Maybe you do love him. And I didn't think how hard coming out must have been for you."

"I just want another chance."

Yes, Kevin loved Russel. I accepted that. Even so, that

didn't mean they belonged together. Russel had moved on, and he and Otto were now perfect together.

"But, Kevin," I said, "don't you see? You had your chance. I'm sorry that you blew it, but you did. Now he needs a chance to love Otto."

Kevin let his arms fall to his sides.

"What are you saying?" he whispered.

Suddenly I realized why it had been so essential that I follow Kevin, and why I was conversing with him now.

"I'm saying," I said, "that you need to tell Russel you've changed your mind. That it's over, and that he has no chance with you."

"What? I can't do—"

"And then you need to leave him completely alone!" I went on. "Otto lives eight hundred miles away. As long as Russel thinks you two might still work out, and as long as you're right here in town, he's never going to be able to love Otto. So you need to cut him out of your life completely. It's the only way he'll ever have a chance with Otto, the only way Russel can ever really be happy with him."

"But—" Kevin raised his hands, as if to struggle again. At that moment, however, he caught sight of something behind my back.

"Here he comes!" whispered Kevin. "You have to get out of here!"

I stared at him a moment longer. "You know this is the right thing," I said. "Please. Do it for Russel."

I didn't wait for Kevin to answer, or even look to see his reaction. There wasn't time—Russel might have already spied me as it was. I hustled off into the bushes.

I knew it wasn't right to eavesdrop on Kevin and Russel, so I immediately started trying to work my way around the park and back to my car. Unfortunately, the greenbelt was dark, and the undergrowth thick. Under my shoes, cold mud squished, releasing the smell of wet clay and rotting leaves; it mingled with the strong odor of methane from the swamp. The whole area was impossibly still, almost like time itself had stopped.

That stillness, and the acoustics of the park, made it so I could hear absolutely everything, every whisper and every little gasp, that was going on back at that gazebo, where Russel had just reached Kevin.

"Who was that?" I heard him ask Kevin.

"Huh?" I heard Kevin respond.

"That guy I saw you talking to. Who was it? He looked older." Russel had seen me in Leah's coat, so he'd also mistaken me for a guy. He'd thought the jacket was an overcoat, making me look like a man. In the dark, the epaulets had probably also made my shoulders look broad.

Kevin didn't answer. Was he going to tell Russel the truth, that it had been me? I wasn't sure how I would ever explain why I'd been talking to Kevin, but I supposed I would think of something.

"He *was* older," said Kevin at last. "In his twenties. He was hitting on me. I've seen him here before."

I stopped in the bushes, confused. What was Kevin saying?

Russel was befuddled too. "Kevin, what are you talking about? What do you mean you've 'seen' him here?"

"What do you *think*?" said Kevin. "Russel, relax. I haven't done it that many times."

I turned back toward the gazebo, which I could still make out through the leaves.

Russel and Kevin were both black-and-white silhouettes now, and I could only see Kevin from behind, but his arms hung limply from his sides. He wasn't thrashing against imaginary chains now.

"'That many times'?" said Russel. "Are you serious?"

"Look!" said Kevin. "What'd you want to see me about?"

"Well, I'm confused," said Russel. "Last week you were

all moony-eyed over me. You came out to the whole school so we could be together. Now you tell me you've been out picking up old guys in parks?"

"Well, it's not like we were together then," said Kevin. "And it's not like that has anything to do with us anyway. That's just sex."

Finally, I understood what Kevin was doing. He wasn't just telling Russel that it was over between the two of them, as I had suggested. He was going one step further: he was trying to make Russel hate him. He was telling lies so that Russel would never want to have anything to do with him again. The result would be far more effective than what I had had in mind. If Kevin succeeded, Russel wouldn't even love him anymore. The question was, would Russel truly believe it?

"So it was all lies?" Russel was saying. "When you said you still loved me? You were just messing around?"

"Hey, I'm an athlete," said Kevin superciliously. "It's a game. And this was one game I wanted to win. I lost the first time around, so I wanted a rematch. I wanted to prove I could win. And I did. I got you to pick me over Otto. But that's all it was. Just a game."

This is what I had accused Kevin of. He had said it to Russel like it was the truth, even though I now knew it wasn't. If there had been any doubt in my mind before about whether he really loved Russel, there wasn't anymore. He loved Russel so much he was pretending to hate him, just so Russel could have a real chance with some new guy. What kind of person made a sacrifice like this? Who was really that selfless? Maybe Xena, Warrior Princess, but she is a TV character, not a real person.

I'd been completely wrong about Kevin. He wasn't a selfish weasel. If he ever had been, he had somehow changed in the last eight months. Otto was still right for Russel, and they deserved a chance to see if the relationship could work. Kevin, meanwhile, had once done a very bad thing to Russel, and it was a past mistake that he definitely had to atone for. Still, by stepping aside to make way for Otto, Kevin was making amends, and more. I, meanwhile, was the only one to witness it.

Would Russel see through his ruse? In order for Kevin's impossible sacrifice to work, Russel could never know the truth. He had to believe Kevin's words completely. If he ever learned what Kevin had done for him, Russel would just love him even more.

I was dying to hear what Russel would say, how he would react. Meanwhile, somewhere overhead, the treetops rustled quietly, like the sound of sand slipping down through an hourglass.

*   *   *

I, of course, had my own problems. Even after the episode in the park was over, I wasn't ready to go home, so I went for a walk. Somehow I found myself back on McKenzie Street, the same place where Leah and I had come twice before. It wasn't yet nine, so college students still ambled along the sidewalks, Christmas shopping and stopping into the cafes for late bites to eat.

I was so confused. I liked Leah a lot; I had thought that maybe I could even love her. That said, there are certain lines in life that are firm, that shouldn't ever be crossed, and tolerating bigotry crosses one of those lines. What did it say about me that I would even consider dating a person who asked me to violate my principles? Next she would be asking me to stop dyeing my hair, or to slip out the back door when her friends stopped by. That would mean I was right back to where I had been with my first girlfriend, Terese, with a relationship in hiding. That was not a place that I was ever willing to go to again.

As I neared the end of the street, I saw that Leah's friends Dade, Savannah, and Alexis were back out soliciting donations for their papier-mâché turkey.

This was very stupid on my part. Why hadn't it occurred to me that her friends would be here again? I was all set to spin away in disgust. At the last second, however, something about them caught my eye. I decided to watch them for a moment. I wasn't worried about them recognizing me; I was a good twenty feet away, and they didn't seem like the type who paid too much attention to faces.

They were dancing to the sound of a tinny Christmas carol emanating from one of the storefronts. As the three of them swayed and twirled, the guys passing by on the sidewalk definitely took notice.

How, I wondered, could these possibly be Leah's friends? What was next, letting frat boys stuff donations into their G-strings?

Dade lifted a tiny pink plastic wand and started gently puffing out glimmering soap bubbles. Savannah and Alexis dipped their wands into the container of soap and blew some bubbles of their own. They fluttered out at the passers-by. Dade laughed, motioning people toward the papier-mâché turkey bin. Savannah flirted with a college professor type; he blushed at the attention but dug into his wallet for a contribution.

Okay, so maybe their dancing wasn't overtly sexual. Maybe they were just flirting and having fun, trying to drum up some donations.

They *were* having fun. A lot of it. Good, innocent fun,

all in the name of a legitimate cause.

Suddenly something occurred to me. This scene—the bubbles, the laughing, the twirling to late-night Christmas carols—was exactly what I was asking Leah to give up. If she came out as a lesbian, it was a good bet that she wouldn't be standing on a sidewalk next Thanksgiving, laughing and blowing bubbles at the frat boys with her high school cheerleader-friends. Moreover, this was only one of the many moments that she would have to forfeit. Sure, she'd have her own fun with her new lesbian and lesbian-tolerant friends, but she'd definitely be sacrificing something.

Suddenly Dade looked over at me.

"Min?" she said.

"Oh," I said. I hadn't expected to be recognized. "Yes."

There was no point in trying to evade them now, so I toddled closer.

"Hi, Dade," I said tentatively. "Hi Savannah, hi Alexis. I didn't quite recognize you guys."

"We recognized you!" said Savannah. "How could we not? God, you're all Leah talks about these days."

This surprised me. "Leah talks about me?" I said.

"Yeah," said Dade. "She really likes you. She wants us to like you too." She blew another shimmering chain of bubbles. "She doesn't have to worry about that. Any friend of Leah's is a friend of ours." She held her plastic wand out toward me. "Hey, you wanna blow some bubbles?"

"No," I said. "That's okay. But thanks."

Leah talked about me with her friends, and she wanted me to be friends with them?

I confess, now I was *really* confused.

CHAPTER EIGHT

THE NEXT DAY, SATURDAY, I had another early morning makeup call. Leah didn't show up at the movie set, which was fine with me, because I didn't know what I would say to her if she did. Russel and Otto weren't there either, but I'd expected this, since today was the day when Otto was flying home. I was dying to hear Russel's version of what had happened the night before. Kevin was another no-show.

Makeup and wardrobe dressed me as a zombie again, but for the first time, they didn't transform me into a cheer-leader. Today, I became a zombie-goth, with a coat of smeared black makeup underneath my zombie makeup. It was pretty funny when you thought about it: the idea of some high school student who worshipped death turning into a zombie. I had been stripped of my pom-poms, but at least I got to keep my purple hair at last.

The first scene was back in the computer lab. Brad and Christy, the two movie leads, discover exactly how someone is turning the whole school into zombies. It's an online computer game so mesmerizing that you can't help but play it; but the more you play, the more it drains your soul, until, finally, you turn into a zombie. In other words, Russel had been right about why the students were transforming into zombies, even if I still didn't know exactly who was responsible.

They weren't shooting close-ups, and the whole computer sequence was a special effect that was going to be added later, so I had no idea if the computer game actually looked mesmerizing or not.

The zombie extras, including Gunnar and myself, just had to sit in the back of the computer lab, mindlessly punching at the keyboard. The joke, of course, was that certain kids are so geeky that they're still online even after being turned into zombies.

"They won't let me see the rushes," said Gunnar glumly as we waited for them to get the cameras ready.

"What?" I said.

"The daily rushes. That's the footage that is shot on a

movie in any given day. They show them every night in the school auditorium. I heard one of the production assistants talking about it, and I asked if I could sit in. But they said no. They said only the 'name' actors can see the rush prints."

"I'm sorry to hear that," I said. "Can we talk for a sec?"

He looked up from his blank computer screen. "Definitely."

I elucidated everything that had happened since we'd last spoken.

"I think I understand Leah's point of view," I said. "She's not a bad person. She just doesn't want to have to choose between her friends and being a lesbian. And she *has* been honest with me, more or less. But I just wonder if someone like her and someone like me are a good match. We're in such different places. So I can't decide if we should even be together."

Gunnar stroked his chin, looking uncommonly self-conscious. "That reminds me of this story," he said.

Great, I thought. Suddenly everyone felt the need to tell me a story.

"Every summer my family goes to Echo Lake for vacation," he said. "It's way out in the middle of nowhere."

"Yes, I know," I said. "So?"

"So a few years ago, I decided to go for a walk in the woods. I walked all afternoon, way up into the mountains. I could tell the trail wasn't used very often, but I kept walking anyway. Finally, I decided to turn around. But as I was hiking back to the lake, I came to this fork in the trail. I didn't remember a fork in the trail! I started to panic. Which way had I come? How did I get home? I knew I had to choose, but both trails looked exactly the same to me."

"So what did you do?" I asked.

"I knew I had the answer somewhere inside me. I *had* come this way before, right? So I relaxed my brain and centered myself, and I tried to cast my mind backward. I stared at both trails until I thought I knew which one was right. Finally, I looked at the trail on the right and thought, That's the one. So that's the one I went down."

"And it was the right one," I said. "Gunnar, I'm not sure—"

"No!" said Gunnar. "I'd picked the *wrong* trail! Before I knew it, I'd walked right into this patch of nettles. And that's not all! I ended up all covered in ticks. And later, I got sick, and I was certain that I'd contracted Lyme disease."

I stared at him. "What are you saying? You picked the wrong trail?"

"Did I?" said Gunnar cryptically. "*Did* I pick the wrong trail? I'm here, aren't I?"

I glowered at him. "What's that supposed to mean?"

"Well, I obviously made it home, right? I lived, right?"

"But what about the nettles and ticks and Lyme disease?"

"Oh, sure," said Gunnar. "I wish I'd picked that other path first. But at least I picked one. Because if I hadn't, I'd still be standing up in those woods."

I finally saw Gunnar's point. Making a choice, any choice, is better than standing around dithering forever. I had to either give it a try with Leah, or not. If I did choose Leah, I had to give it my all. In the end, I'd either learn she was right for me, or I'd end up covered in ticks and nettle stings.

I was now completely convinced that Gunnar showed no signs of Asperger's syndrome whatsoever.

"That's a good story," I admitted.

"It better be," said Gunnar. "It's the second time in two days that I've told it."

According to Gunnar, I just needed to make a decision. That, however, was easier said than done. *Did* I want to give it a try with Leah? That was the real question. Did I want to see if being with her led to ticks and nettles, or did I want to just walk away now with my integrity intact?

The very next scene was another one in a school hallway. This time, all I had to do was lurch disjointedly around while two zombie-cheerleaders pantomimed some mocking of my goth wardrobe; nearby, a zombie-jock was thrashing on a zombie-nerd. In the foreground, meanwhile, Brad and Christy had some dialogue together. I wasn't really listening. I was still thinking about what to do with Leah.

"There's only one person who had access to those computer labs after-hours!" said the actor playing Brad.

"Who?" said the actress playing Christy.

Suddenly the actor playing the janitor stepped into the scene behind Brad and Christy.

"So you finally figured it out, did you?" said the janitor.

"*You?*" said Christy. "You're the one who's been turning the whole school into zombies? But why?"

I looked directly over at the actors, even though we weren't supposed to do that while the cameras were rolling. I couldn't help myself, and could only hope that I was off camera at the time. I just couldn't believe that the *janitor* was the culprit. How was that possible? I had been certain it was the nurse or the captain of the football team—anyone but the janitor! Having the janitor do it was a total cliché!

"I know why," announced Brad. "It's because he's jealous! Don't you remember those football trophies we found down near the furnace? They were his. For him, high school was the Glory Days. But what has he done since then? Nothing but mop floors and grow slowly older!"

"Not for much longer!" said the janitor. "Because I'm

not just stealing your souls! I'm using them to grow younger!"

Oh, man! I thought. The janitor was doing all this because he was a resentful aging jock and was now trying to appropriate the teenagers' youth? That was even *more* of a cliché! I also couldn't help but wonder why it was Brad who succeeded in figuring everything out while Christy stood there looking clueless. Because the screenwriter was a guy, that's why. Just as I'd expected, *Attack of the Soul-Sucking Brain Zombies* was no homage to monster movies—it was just plain bad writing.

I couldn't believe I'd been wrong about the janitor. I'd been so *certain*.

Could it be, I thought, that I'd been wrong about a few other things as well?

After the shoot, I drove straight to Leah's house. I was still wearing my zombie-goth makeup, but I didn't care. Her mother opened the door.

"Hi," I said. "Is Leah here?"

"Oh," she said. "You're from the zombie movie, right?"

"How'd you know?"

"Just a guess. She's up in her room."

Upstairs, I knocked on Leah's door. She told me to come in, and I entered and closed the door firmly behind me.

She was sitting at her computer. When she saw my makeup, she laughed.

"A zombie-goth!" she said. "That's *hilarious*!"

I didn't even smile.

"I think I might love you," I said evenly.

She stopped laughing. "Yeah," she said. "I think I might love you too."

"I want to give this a try."

Leah crossed and sat on the bed. "Me too."

"I can understand how you don't want to just throw your old life away," I said. "I wouldn't either. And I won't make you. It's okay with me if you don't want to come out, and I won't tell your friends that I'm bi, or that we're a couple."

"Thanks, Min. I really appreciate that."

"But," I said, "I have a couple of conditions for you too."

"Okay. That's only fair."

"One, no more homophobic comments or jokes, ever. If your friends make them, we speak up. I don't care if it looks suspicious. I won't be around that, and I won't tolerate it. It makes me feel too horrible. Same goes for racism or any other kind of prejudice."

Leah nodded. I think she knew I had a point.

"Two," I said. "I won't disappear or go into hiding. If I'm going to be a part of your life, I want to *be* a part of your life. That includes spending time with your friends. If you like them, somehow I'll learn to like them. But I won't do the whole relationship-in-hiding thing. I'm not going to disappear into the shadows, not for you, not for anyone, ever again. Agreed?"

"Agreed."

I thought for a second, but realized that I'd said everything I'd come to say.

"Well, then," I said at last. "I think we've effectively completed our negotiations." I tapped my foot. "Now if only we had some way to seal this agreement. Some way to consummate the arrangement."

A smile tugged at Leah's lips. "Yeah, some symbolic gesture."

I flitted closer to the bed. "We could sign some kind of document."

"Too formal," said Leah. "Besides, I don't have any clean paper."

I sat down next to her on the bed. It squeaked. "We could shake hands."

"That's an idea," she said. "I like that it's physical. But I still don't think that's quite right."

"Hmmm." I turned to face her on the bed; the mattress sagged, so we were being drawn together. "Well, what else could we do? How else do people seal these things?" I leaned closer still, until my lips were almost touching hers.

Then they touched.

We kissed.

Before we could get too far, however, Leah suddenly stiffened.

"What?" I said.

"I just realized! Dade, Alexis, and Savannah are on their way over here right now!"

In other words, the terms of our agreement were about to be put to their first test!

CHAPTER NINE

DADE, SAVANNAH, AND ALEXIS descended upon Leah's bedroom like a herd of elephants—well, bulimic elephants wearing $150 perfumes. Leah's room was once again reminiscent of a crowded elevator, one I suddenly wished I'd never set foot in.

"Hey, Min," said Savannah. By this time, I'd washed off my zombie-goth makeup.

"Hey, guys," I said. Leah's friends made me nervous, but I confess I wasn't getting any weirdness from them now, about my purple hair or being Asian or anything.

"What are you guys up to?" asked Leah.

"It's a Saturday night," said Dade. "What else? Pore strips!"

"Pardon me?" I said.

Dade held up a plastic bag from a nearby drugstore. "Pore strips! You know, those little sticky strips that you put on your face, let dry, and rip 'em off, so they suck out your blackheads?"

Leah looked chagrined. "It's kind of a tradition with us."

"Yeah," said Alexis, "and afterward, we tell ghost stories and eat cookie dough ice cream and braid each other's hair!"

"Either that or go out and get stoned," said Savannah.

Everyone laughed. I did too. I concede that Leah's friends could sometimes be funny.

Dade hauled out four boxes of pore strips. The directions called for washing our faces prior to application, so that's what we did. Then everyone peeled the backs off and stuck the strips to their cheeks, noses, and foreheads. They smelled clean, like alcohol and paste.

"Now what?" I said.

"Now we wait for them to dry," said Dade.

"And talk," said Savannah. "Usually we play Truth or Dare. Min, you're first."

"Savannah!" said Dade. "Don't be a bitch." To me, she said, "Savannah's just kidding. Well, about the Truth or Dare part, not about the talking part."

I laughed. "It's fine. You can ask whatever you want." It

was fine. Leah and I had an agreement. I was determined to be part of her life with her friends, and I wasn't going to tolerate their homophobia. Before this evening was over, I was going to find out if Leah could really accept that.

"I heard that Declan McDonnell is starring in that movie you guys are working on," said Dade. "Is that true?" This was the actor playing Brad. Russel had mentioned that he'd once been on some television show, but I had no idea that anyone else actually knew who he was.

"Oh," I said. "Yes, it is."

"God!" said Alexis. "He's so hot!"

Savannah smacked Leah on the arm. "Why didn't you tell us! I would have done it if I'd known *he* was in it. Have you *seen* him?"

"Oh, sure," said Leah. "He's in most of the scenes. But we're not supposed to talk to him."

"What's he like?" asked Savannah.

"I have no idea," I admitted. "I haven't really paid any attention."

"You *haven't?*" said Savannah. "Why not?"

"I don't know," I said lamely. "I guess he's not really my type."

"Like I said," said Leah, trying to bail me out, "we're not really supposed to talk to the stars."

This was not going well. How was I supposed to spend

time with Leah's friends if I couldn't find any common ground?

"What is your type?" Dade asked me.

"Huh?" I said.

"Guys. What kind of guys do you like?"

Leah looked at me. I think she wondered how I was going to answer this particular question. Still, I *am* bi; I could answer it more or less truthfully.

"Oh, you know," I said with a shrug. "Just guys. Are these supposed to itch?" I meant the strips plastered all over my face.

"Yeah," said Leah. "When it dries, the skin gets all tight. That means it's working."

"No, seriously," said Dade to me. "Sensitive guys? Nah, you'd so scare 'em off. I bet you're into bad boys, right? God, I *love* bad boys!"

What was I supposed to say to that? I hated macho jerks and the vapid teenage girls who made them popular. That said, if I started hyperventilating about sexism, Leah's friends were certain to think I was a total freak. If I kept that up, it wouldn't be long until they started asking questions about Leah too.

Right then I realized that there was a big contradiction inherent in my agreement with Leah: I'd said I wouldn't out myself or Leah, but that I wanted to spend time with her and her friends. However, if I did spend time with them, it was only a matter of time before I more or less outed myself.

If I was completely honest about things, that is.

I glanced at Leah. She looked genuinely scared, like she'd fallen down a deep well into ice-cold water, and no one except me knew she was there. Would I abandon her at this crucial time?

Wait, I thought: Leah's friends' stopping by was supposed to be a test of Leah, not me. This was ironic.

Finally, I said to Dade, "Well, yes. I like a good bad boy now and then."

"Yeah, I bet," mewed Savannah.

I sighed dreamily—or as dreamily as I know how. "I like it when a guy just, you know, takes *charge*," I said. "Makes *decisions*. I can't stand those wimpy guys that are always staring at you with puppy dog eyes, waiting to see what it is *you* want."

"Oh, God yeah!" said Savannah. "So milquetoast."

What was I doing? What I was saying went against everything I believed about guys *and* girls. This was like the end of that movie *The Graduate* and a million other movies, only in reverse. Rather than stand up and boldly proclaim my love for Leah, damn the consequences, I was doing the exact opposite. I was pretending to be a different person completely. This, however, was more or less what I had promised Leah.

"I like a guy with dirty fingernails," I said. "And a light sheen of sweat on his back. All these women who complain about razor burn? I like razor burn! It means a guy's got testosterone. And I like boxers, not briefs, and don't even get me started on bikini briefs. And no hair gel! What is that about? Hair gel is for girls, not guys."

"Amen, sister!" said Dade. "Down with metrosexuals."

Leah looked at me. There were tears in her eyes. She knew exactly what I was doing—that in a way I *was* proclaiming my love for her, just as boldly as the end of *The Graduate* and all those other movies. No, I wasn't sacrificing everything to do the right thing, like Xena, Warrior Princess. Then again, I didn't have an evil past to atone for. Even so, I was still making a serious compromise. Leah, meanwhile, was the only person who knew exactly what sacrifice I was making, which is exactly the way it should have been.

"Lousy penmanship!" howled Alexis. "That's a sign that a man is a real *animal*. I mean, how many gorillas are out there writing novellas?"

"I like a guy with a rumbly voice," said Savannah. "I feel like I can feel it all the way down in my gut."

As her friends fanned the flames that I had lit, I sat down on the bed next to Leah. Because of the saggy springs, our thighs touched again. She didn't look at me, and I didn't look at her, but we both knew what each other was thinking.

It's funny how complicated life can be. The only way to stick to my principles was to not stick to my principles? I never would have predicted this.

"Okay!" Dade announced at last. "It's time for the pore strip stripping!"

"It's going to hurt, isn't it?" I said.

"A little," said Savannah. "But it's like a Band-Aid. The faster you do it, the less it hurts."

"Ready?" said Dade. "Nose strip first!"

"Ready," we all said.

"Pull!"

We pulled.

It only hurt a little.

"Compare!" commanded Dade.

"Compare?" I said.

"Blackheads," said Leah, nodding down to her own strip. Little black and brown spikes, like thorns, poked up from the surface of the white plastic.

"Oh my God, you can *see* them!" I had never used these pore strips before—had never even *considered* using them—so I'd had no idea how they worked.

Everyone laughed—not at me, but with me, at my obviously sincere amazement.

"*Compare!*" Dade repeated.

We compared. Savannah "won" with the thickest, darkest blackheads.

"Oooooooo!" said Dade.

"That is so disgusting," said Alexis.

"I can't believe that all came off of my nose!" wailed Savannah.

"Oh, Savannah, you *always* say that!" said Leah.

"Ready forehead strips!" announced Dade.

"Now here's where Savannah gets her revenge," said Leah to me. "Alexis always loses the forehead strip."

I pulled, but at the same time I was thinking about all of this. I was engaged in a pore-strip competition with a bunch of cheerleading airheads. Never in a million years would I have expected this either. Was life strange or what?

The even weirder part is, I was actually having fun.

Afterward, Dade, Savannah, and Alexis wanted to go to a party. Leah and I, however, bowed out. We lied and told them we were going to rendezvous with some boys from *Attack of the Soul-Sucking Brain Zombies*.

We went for a drive and ended up on McKenzie Street. It was after nine now, and all the shops had closed.

"That was a very interesting evening," I said to Leah.

"Thanks again," she said.

"Hey, a promise is a promise."

When we reached the end of the stretch of shops and cafes on McKenzie Street, Leah pointed down a side road.

"Off into uncharted territory?" she said.

"How appropriate," I said.

In a couple of blocks, we wandered onto the college campus. Most of the lights were off. As we walked through the grounds, I looked around at the darkness. I remembered the night before, when I'd walked through that park to get to Kevin, and how the darkness had reminded me of a black-and-white movie. It still did, but in this light, I suddenly saw shades and textures that I hadn't noticed the night before. The stones in the pavement were almost white. The shadows under the rhododendrons were a deep, dark black. However, everywhere else I looked—the flat expanses of grass, the trunks of the trees, the ivy-covered brick buildings—I saw a thousand shades of gray.

I reached out and slipped my hand into Leah's. Her hand was big and warm, covering mine like a glove. We passed students in the dark, mostly in the distance, but Leah didn't pull away. Of course I was still wearing Leah's jacket, so people may have thought we were a girl and a short guy in an overcoat. I didn't mind. In a way, it somehow seemed like a good compromise.

"Do you think college is really that different from high school?" asked Leah.

"I do," I said. "I think it's completely different." I wasn't sure if this was true, but it felt true at the time.

Eventually, we reached the end of the official campus, but we forged on until we came to the football stadium. This late at night, it was deserted, but there was trash all around, programs and Styrofoam cups, making me think there had been a game there earlier in the evening. Someone had left the front gate unlocked.

"Let's go inside," I said.

"Okay," said Leah.

Inside, the lights were all turned off, and the stands were empty. The air smelled of popcorn and moldy paint and frost. The chalk lines on the field glowed a pale white in the moonlight. It was strange to be in such a vast open space and have there be no movement and no sound. Still, I could somehow sense the lingering presence of the people who had been here earlier, afterimages in the cinema of time.

We walked to the very middle of the field. I stepped in front of Leah. Her face glowed too, a second moon to light the dark. Her lips were the softest gray I had ever seen, and her eyes were as deep and endless as the starlit sky.

Here at last we could finally say what we couldn't say in front of Dade and the others.

"I love you," Leah whispered.

"I love you too," I whispered back.

We met in the kiss to end all kisses.

Up in the stands, the roar of a thousand invisible spectators cheered us on.

CHAPTER TEN

THE NEXT MORNING, MY mom was reading the newspaper at the kitchen table.

"You were out late last night," she said. "Have fun?"

"Yes," I said. I grabbed a banana from the fruit basket. "I left my cave. Apparently my head isn't so big yet that I can't still fit through the exit."

She perked up. "Really?"

"Really." It was all I could do not to point out that her ridiculous headband made her hair look like she was wearing a shower cap.

"So," asked my mom. "How was it on the outside?"

"Nice," I said thoughtfully. "Airy."

"Well, good for you! But now I have to tell you the other story my mother used to tell me, about a fellow who wandered around aimlessly and refused to take a stand on anything."

"No, thanks, Mom," I said, withdrawing to my room to eat my banana and IM Leah.

That night, I visited Russel. It was time to finally come clean about everything that had been going on with Leah.

"So," I said.

"So," he said sheepishly, his eyes downcast. "There's been a lot going on in my life lately."

"Really?" I said. "Like what?" I liked that he thought he'd been keeping secrets from me.

He told me everything that had been going on with him and Kevin and Otto, and finally filled me in on that night in the park with Kevin. I just pursed my face, and laughed, and scowled, and acted like I was hearing everything for the very first time.

"You've had a busy couple of weeks," I said when Russel was finished.

"Yeah," he said. "Sorry I haven't kept you up-to-date."

"Here's the thing. I haven't exactly kept you up-to-date either."

"You haven't?"

I shook my head, and started to tell him about Leah.

"I had no idea!" he said. Unlike Russel, I really had been keeping secrets.

I recounted all the times that he had inadvertently helped get the two of us together.

"Ha!" he said. "I'm a matchmaker, and I didn't even know it!"

I told him the rest of the story, including the part about what had happened with Leah's friends the night before.

He stared at me for a second.

"What?" I said, embarrassed.

He shook his head. "Nothing. Nothing at all." Still, I knew what he was thinking. I'd surprised him. That was okay: I'd surprised myself too.

"Just one question about all this," I said.

"Yeah?" said Russel.

"What the hell is a brain zombie?"

"You didn't—?"

"Nope. I did learn it was the janitor who was turning the kids into zombies."

"See! Told you so."

I deliberately ignored him. "And I learned that he was doing it with that stupid computer game. But I never heard exactly what a brain zombie is."

"Maybe it means a zombie of the mind. Someone who

becomes a zombie, or not, because of the people around him."

"Maybe so," I said, because it seemed as good an answer as any.

That Monday at school, Russel, Gunnar, and I were strolling down the hallway, and we stumbled upon that poster, the one calling for extras on *Attack of the Soul-Sucking Brain Zombies*.

"Damn," said Russel. "Something just occurred to me." He turned to me. "I owe you ten bucks."

"What?" I said.

"Don't you remember? When we first saw this poster? You bet that if we did the movie, we'd all have completely different experiences?"

"Yeah," muttered Gunnar. "*Someone* was in a bad mood that day."

"The fact is," said Russel to me, "you were right." He thought for a second. "*Boy*, were you right! Talk about completely different experiences!" He laughed and started digging for his wallet.

I thought about everything that had happened over the last few weeks—the part that Russel knew about, and the part that he didn't.

I placed my hand on his wrist. "It's okay. I didn't win that bet."

He looked up at me.

"Sure, different things happened to each of us." I said. "But we were together too, in more ways than one. Even when we weren't together, we were together, you know?"

"Oh." Russel thought again. "Well, in that case, you can pay *me*!"

I laughed.

"No," said Russel. "Seriously! Pay up!"

Only now did he finally laugh.

"So what's next?" said Gunnar.

"What do you mean?" I asked him.

"Oh, you know us. Seems like we're always in the middle of something. So what's next?"

This was a very good question. I was quite looking forward to the answer. It would mean, of course, another beginning. Before you can introduce a new beginning, however, you must first finish what you were already doing, and that means you must clearly and definitively have . . .

THE END

SPLIT SCREEN

ATTACK OF THE SOUL-SUCKING BRAIN ZOMBIES

BRENT HARTINGER

HarperTempest
An Imprint of HarperCollins*Publishers*

HarperTempest is an imprint of HarperCollins Publishers.

www.harperteen.com

Library of Congress Cataloging-in-Publication Data
Hartinger, Brent.
Split screen / by Brent Hartinger. — 1st ed.
p.   cm.
Summary: Two books in one tell of sixteen-year-old friends
Russel, who is gay, and Min, who is bisexual, as they face separate
romantic troubles while working as extras on the set of a horror
movie.
ISBN-10: 0-06-082408-5 (trade bdg.)
ISBN-13: 978-0-06-082408-2 (trade bdg.)
ISBN-10: 0-06-082409-3 (lib bdg.)
ISBN-13: 978-0-06-082409-9 (lib bdg.)
[1.   Homosexuality—Fiction. 2.   Bisexuality—Fiction.
3. Horror films—Fiction. 4. Motion pictures—Production and
direction—Fiction. 5. Actors and actresses—Fiction. 6. Family
life—Fiction.] I. Title.
PZ7.H2635Spl 2007   2006029872
[Fic]—dc22   CIP
                                                         AC

Typography by Joel Tippie
1 2 3 4 5 6 7 8 9 10
❖
First Edition

For Michael Jensen,
who is all the protection I need against zombies

Special thanks to Tom Baer, Tim Cathersal, Harold Hartinger,
Danny Oryshchyn, and James Venturini.

CHAPTER ONE

I WAS STANDING FAR from daylight, deep in an echoing corridor of stone. The air was dry and dusty, and all around me, lifeless bodies lurched and groaned.

Then my best friend Gunnar motioned to me and my other best friend Min from over by a bulletin board next to a row of lockers. "Russ! Min!" he said. "You have to come see this!"

I was standing in the concrete hallways of Robert L. Goodkind High School, surrounded by sleep-deprived high school students. Hey, it was 8 A.M.—what'd you expect?

Why the zombies-in-a-crypt imagery? Well, that's just me, Russel Middlebrook—always trying to be cute. But it also had something to do with the flier that my best friend Gunnar had seen on that bulletin board.

ZOMBIES WANTED! it read. Below that in smaller print it said:

> Teenagers needed as extras for upcoming horror film, *Attack of the Soul-Sucking Brain Zombies*, to be produced in local area. Come let us turn you into gruesome, monstrous zombies!

Then there was contact info.

"They're filming a zombie movie in town, and they need teenagers to be extras, isn't that *cool*, we should totally do it!" Gunnar was saying, all without taking a breath. I hadn't seen him this excited since he found lamprey eels in the creek near our houses.

Let's face it, Gunnar was kind of a geek. But I loved that he got so obsessive about things, sometimes to the exclusion of everything else. He was originally from Norway, which has nothing to do with anything, but he has this slight accent (which people used to make fun of him for), so I figured it was something you should know.

"Aren't they kind of late for zombies?" Min said. "Halloween was two weeks ago." She was right. It was already the second week in November.

"They're *filming* the movie," Gunnar said. "Not releasing it."

"And what's a 'brain zombie'?" I asked.

"I know," Min said. "Brain zombies? That doesn't even make sense."

"I'm sure it's explained in the script!" Gunnar said loudly. "Look, do you guys want to do it or not? I know Em will!" Em was Gunnar's girlfriend, who was just as geeky as he was (in a good way).

"I don't know," Min said. She was the school egghead, but she wasn't your typical Chow Mein Brain (her term, not mine). For one thing, she wasn't at all shy and submissive. She was actually pretty in-your-face. Example: she had recently put purple streaks in her hair. And she was bi and open about it. Still, she loved monster movies, so I would have thought she would have wanted to be in one.

I looked at her. "What's wrong?"

"Huh?" she said. "Nothing."

But I like to think I'm a pretty observant guy, and I knew she was lying. Min was lonely. She'd had bad luck lately, with both guys *and* girls. I could relate. I'm gay, and before I came out the previous spring, I had felt like the only gay person in the universe. But I had a boyfriend now, this great guy named Otto (who, unfortunately, lived eight hundred miles away).

"This zombie thing could be fun," I said to Min.

"Yes, maybe." She stared past me, down the hall.

"We'd all be together, at least."

Min met my gaze. "No, we won't. Not really."

"Yeah, we will!" Gunnar said. "Why wouldn't we be?"

Min sighed. "Because people are always alone. Sure, we're 'together,' but not really. We all might be doing the same thing, being zombie extras on this movie set. But we wouldn't ever really know what the others are thinking or feeling. It'd be a completely different experience for each of us."

Needless to say, not only was Min in-your-face, she could also be full of it. But at least now I knew I'd been right about her feeling lonely.

"Please," I said. "Zombie guts are zombie guts are zombie guts." This was a play on that poem, "A rose is a rose is a rose." Trust me, I didn't go around quoting Gertrude Stein to just anyone. But I knew Min, being full of it, would get the reference.

"Are they?" she said. "Zombie guts might mean one thing to you, but something completely different to me. Even if we were always together, which we won't be, it wouldn't be the same experience at all. I bet you ten dollars that if we do this, we'll have completely different experiences."

"Yeah, but that doesn't mean—"

Suddenly Gunnar erupted (and interrupted). *"Enough with the boring philosophy talk!"* he said. "Are we going to do the zombie movie or not?"

"Oh, calm down," I said matter-of-factly. "Extras in a horror movie? Of *course* the three of us are going to do something as cool as *that*."

So a couple of days later, Min, Gunnar, Em, and I trundled off to this informational meeting for extras who wanted to be in *Attack of the Soul-Sucking Brain Zombies*. It was held in the afternoon in the auditorium of a local high school, one that had been closed for the year for remodeling. About forty other teenagers shifted uncomfortably on squeaky wooden seats. I hardly recognized anyone—almost everybody else must have come from the other high schools in the surrounding area. The somewhat meager turnout surprised me, since I couldn't imagine any teenager *not* wanting to play a zombie in a real movie. Then again, I'd learned long ago—and had been reminded *so* many times in my life!—that what interested me didn't necessarily interest other people my age.

There were a few wannabe divas from the schools' various drama clubs, but most of the other people who'd showed up were pretty clearly geeks. The teenage zombies in this

movie were going to be doubly scary: in addition to mangled faces and intestines hanging out, they would all have an irritating knowledge of calculus and old *Star Trek* reruns.

"Carrots and peas," Gunnar said out of the blue.

"What?" I said.

"That's what movie extras are supposed to say to make it look like they're really talking," he explained. "They don't say real words, they just repeat the phrase 'carrots and peas' over and over again."

"Really?" Em said. "That's very interesting!"

"The thing I don't get," I said, "is why they didn't film this movie over the summer."

6 "Lots of reasons," Gunnar said. "Maybe they didn't have their financing in place. Maybe they needed the outdoor shots to be autumn-specific. That's the thing about filmmaking—you need to be flexible."

"But most of their extras are high school students," I pointed out. "During the week, we'll be in class all day!"

"So that's when they'll shoot the scenes that don't need extras in the background."

Gunnar had obviously done his research. I knew right then that he had suddenly become an expert on absolutely everything related to making movies.

A few minutes later, two guys plodded out onstage.

They looked younger than I would have thought, like college students (freshmen, not seniors). I wondered if they were extras who had gotten lost backstage.

Then they introduced themselves as the producer and director of *Attack of the Soul-Sucking Brain Zombies*.

"In Hollywood, being young is a *good* thing," Gunnar whispered.

"So," the producer said, "you guys want to be zombies, huh?"

The crowd immediately whooped it up. They didn't care that the producer and the director were only shaving twice a week. They wanted to be zombies!

The producer and director smirked at each other. They were young, but cocky, and we were reacting exactly the way they wanted.

The producer went on to explain how they would be filming *Attack of the Soul-Sucking Brain Zombies* at that school for the next three weeks, but that they'd only need us extras on the weekends and on the Friday of Thanksgiving break (we'd all get Thanksgiving itself off).

"During the week," the director said, "we'll be shooting the scenes that don't need extras in the background."

Gunnar grinned at me like the Cheshire cat who had just spoken the words "I told you so." I rolled my eyes.

The producer told us we'd be playing high school students, but that over the course of the filming we'd be gradually turning into zombies. He also mentioned the "rules" of the set, which I won't bore you with here, except to say that under no circumstances were we supposed to talk to the stars. I couldn't help but notice that the producer was talking as if we'd all already agreed to be zombie extras. Which I guess we had. But still, isn't that one of the techniques they use to get people to join cults?

Finally, the producer asked us if we had any questions.

Gunnar's hand shot up. "Will you be making your own fake blood, or will you be buying it premade?" he asked. "Because you can make great fake blood with nothing but corn syrup and red food coloring!"

Not one teenager in the auditorium laughed at Gunnar's question—which tells you a lot about the geekiness level of the gathering.

The producer looked at the director.

"Well," the director said, "we'll have to leave the technical questions for our special effects supervisor, who isn't here tonight."

Disappointment settled over the room like a blanket.

"Does anyone have any schedule-related questions?" the producer said brightly. "Anything like that?"

Min raised her hand. "How much will we be paid?" she asked, and Gunnar shot her a foul look.

The producer chuckled. "Fair enough. Well, this is a nonunion production, so you won't be paid according to the SAG scale."

"SAG stands for the Screen Actors Guild," Gunnar whispered.

For the record, I was already bored with Gunnar's knowledge of moviemaking.

"But you'll each get fifty-eight dollars a day," the producer went on. "And we will, of course, provide meals."

We were going to be paid fifty-eight dollars a day? This was *great* news! After all, we hadn't come for the pay, but for the experience (or, according to Min, for all of our separate, individual, and completely unique experiences!). We were also there to keep Gunnar's head from exploding.

"So that's all for tonight," the producer said. "I've got some release forms that you need to sign, and you need to have your parents sign if you're under the age of—"

Suddenly a mangled, green-skinned man burst from backstage. Tattered clothing dangled from his angular body; mustard-yellow eyes stared blankly forward. He stumbled, zombielike, toward the producer and director, who had not yet noticed him.

Down in the seats, we would-be extras gasped in surprise.

The producer and director jerked around to face the zombie. But it was too late to run. The creature was upon them, grabbing the director's arm and twisting it right out of its socket. The director screamed, and blood spurted as if from a hose. Meanwhile, the zombie started munching on the dismembered arm, actually biting off pieces of flesh. The producer started to run, so the zombie threw the arm aside and went after him, catching him and clawing at his chest with dirt-caked fingernails. The producer howled as bloody streaks oozed out into his shirt and a clear liquid soaked the crotch of his pants.

10 Needless to say, the crowd went absolutely nuts—both laughing and screaming hysterically, since nobody was completely sure exactly what was going on. All I know is we were transfixed, which I'm sure was the reaction the producer and director had intended.

Once the zombie had reduced both the producer and the director to quivering masses of flesh and little jets of pulsing blood, the creature lumbered off backstage again.

The whole room fell silent again as we gaped at the now-immobile corpses up onstage.

Then suddenly the producer and director leaped up onto their feet, laughing and slapping each other on the

back. The director's dismembered arm had been fake, and he pulled his real arm up out of his shirt. (Presumably, the wet stain in the producer's crotch had been faked too—a very realistic touch!)

"Okay, so we lied!" the producer said. "The special effects supervisor *is* here tonight!" He winked in Gunnar's direction. "And for the record, we do make our own blood!"

The crowd roared again. Meanwhile, the producer introduced the "zombie," who came back out onstage to explain everything that they had just done to make it look like we had witnessed a vicious monster attack.

Okay, so Gunnar had been right. This whole movie thing was going to be incredibly cool!

Finally, the meeting really came to an end (no more zombie attacks). The producer and director passed out the release forms, and we were free to go.

We were working our way to the back of the auditorium with the rest of the crowd and were almost to the exit when I suddenly spotted a very familiar face.

Kevin Land.

Long story short: Kevin had been my first boyfriend, this baseball jock with dark hair and an impish grin. He wore a

light blue work sweatshirt that had been spattered with red paint (and *boy*, did he fill it out nicely!). Basically, Kevin was hotter than jalapeños. He was also sweet and gentle and oh-so-cuddly.

Sounds like the perfect boyfriend, right? Well, he was, except for one small thing. I came out of the closet at school, and he didn't. Which sounds like a small deal, except it's not. When two guys are dating and only one of them is out of the closet, eventually the in-the-closet one will be forced to choose between the closet and the other guy. In my case, Kevin chose the closet, and he'd been a real jerk about it. In other words, he wasn't so sweet and gentle and cuddly after all. So I had no choice but to dump him. Which isn't to say I didn't miss him, sometimes a lot.

I know this is confusing. The point is, I now had this great new boyfriend, Otto, so the whole thing was moot anyway.

I'd seen Kevin since we broke up, at school and stuff. But he and I ran in different circles—*really* different circles. Basically, he was popular, and I wasn't. Which meant that while I had *seen* him, I hadn't ever talked to him. But somehow running into him here seemed different than seeing him at school.

"Kevin?" I said. I'm pretty sure I looked happy, in spite of everything.

"Kevin!" Min said. She didn't look or sound happy at all. On the contrary, she seemed annoyed.

He nodded and grinned—the impish smile I mentioned earlier. "Hey, Russel," he said. "Hey, Min." But it was like he was deliberately avoiding looking at her.

"Uh, what are you doing here?" I asked him. I figured he had to have been waiting for someone—a friend, a tutor, maybe even (gulp) a new boyfriend.

"Well, I wanted to be a zombie."

"Is that *right*?" This was actually Min, not me.

"Yeah," Kevin said. "That was pretty cool, what they did, huh?"

"Huh?" I said. "Oh, yeah, it was. So you came here to be a movie extra too?"

"Yeah, I saw that poster in the hallway, and I thought it looked really interesting."

"What a *coincidence*," Min said.

I, meanwhile, was thinking, This is not possible! Kevin was going to be in *Attack of the Soul-Sucking Brain Zombies* too? Talk about the dead rising up out of the grave!

But now we were both working on the same project. So suddenly Kevin Land was talking to me again. This was the last thing in the world I wanted (more or less).

"Russel," Min insisted. "We should go." Gunnar and Em had somehow already passed us and were probably waiting in the parking lot.

"Yeah," I said. "Sure. Well," I said to Kevin. "See you." Min was pulling me away.

"Hey, Russel?" Kevin said. I turned. "We should get together sometime. Just to talk."

Just to talk? Well, what else would we do? (Get your mind out of the gutter!)

"I mean it!" Min said. "We really have to go."

Before I could give Kevin an answer, Min was literally dragging me away. If I hadn't been so stunned by the whole Kevin-suddenly-reappearing thing, I probably would have wondered what the hell had gotten into her.

So Kevin Land was back in my life. I could *not* believe it. At that point, I couldn't imagine anything that would make my life any more complicated.

Then I got home from zombie practice. I walked past the living room, where my parents were taking down the Halloween decorations.

My mom immediately turned to confront me. She was clutching a white candle in the shape of a skull, something that had been set on the fireplace mantel.

"Russel," she whispered, like just saying the word was this great, terrible burden.

My dad looked over at me too. "Russel, please come in here," he said, also choking out the words. "We need to talk." He was holding a paper coffin against his chest like a security blanket.

"Talk?" I said. This wasn't good, but I couldn't exactly walk away. I pushed my way through the strands of fake spiderwebs that hung, partially unpinned, from the arch that led into the living room.

I had barely gotten two feet when my mom suddenly blurted, "Is it true? Are you gay?"

Un-fricking-believable. The exact same day that Kevin had zombied his way back into my life, my parents had somehow also discovered that I'm gay!

CHAPTER TWO

MY PARENTS. OH, GOD, how do I explain my parents?

My dad first, since he's easier.

He's an investment counselor. That means he meets with people and helps them figure out how to invest their money.

That's pretty much it.

I don't mean to be mean. But his job is his life. He is not a complicated person. He just loves his job—stocks and bonds and plastic binders and rubber bands and PowerPoint projections. He's big and friendly and a little goofy-looking. I used to joke he looked like Mr. Clean, except with no earring and more hair.

My mom, meanwhile, *is* a complicated person. She works as the office manager at a dentist's office, but that's

just her job. She does a million other things—gourmet cooking, handball, volunteer work with disabled kids, bonsai gardening. As for the rest, she's a bundle of contradictions. She clips fifty-cent coupons, but she'll spend five hundred dollars on a pair of shoes. She never yells, but she's often angry. She looks fantastic—trim and sophisticated—but all she ever eats is dessert.

Mostly, she just really, really, really, really cares what other people think about her. Go back to the bonsai tree thing for a second. Bonsai trees look great, but it sure doesn't come easy. They have to be trimmed and wired and kept in tiny pots with bound roots. The trees probably don't like it much, but then again, it's not about the trees. It's all about the way they look, the fact that they're perfect.

My mom is like that with everything. It had something to do with her upbringing. Her father died young, leaving her mom and brother and her very poor. But according to my mom, being poor doesn't mean you can't have dignity. I have no idea what this means exactly, but it has something to do with not having a couch on your front porch.

Anyway, since I was her son, I was a reflection on her. So she really, really, really, really cared what people thought of me. Good grades were nonnegotiable, and fluorescent green shoelaces were an offense against God and

nature. Even worse, they were "tacky," which is apparently the worst thing in the world you can be.

In other words, look perfect. Be a bonsai tree.

Needless to say, my parents and I didn't have a lot in common.

A house. Some DNA.

That's about it. Sometimes it was like they lived on one continent and I lived on another. Sure, we talked, but more like it was on the phone and the connection was horrible. Plus the customs and practices on their continent were just so different from the customs and practices on mine. To say anything complicated required so much background information that after a while it just became easier to never say anything real at all.

"Did you brush your teeth?"

"Yes."

"Did you pick up grapes when you were at the store?"

"No, you said not to get them if they were too expensive."

"Okay, love you! Let's be sure and talk again in three months."

Still, this is where things get complicated. Sure, my parents and I didn't have a lot in common, but they *were* my parents, and I did love them. They had done their best rais-

ing me, which was pretty darn good. I mean, they'd never chained me up in a closet (although that's setting the bar kind of low, isn't it?).

In all seriousness, my parents had always looked out for me. I think about all the buckets of vomit my mom had cleaned up when I was sick. How fun was that? Or the time when I was eight and I slammed my finger in the car door, and my dad held me in his arms all the way to the emergency room.

My parents had also taught me how to get by in the world, to look both ways before crossing the street, and not to jam the screwdriver into the wall outlet. They'd taught me the difference between right and wrong—that it wasn't okay to lie and steal, or stare at the man with no nose.

My parents were good, decent people. They gave money to charity, and they voted. They didn't litter. They didn't make fun of the homeless, or laugh at insult humor, or tolerate racial stereotypes. And they loved me—I had never before doubted that.

Which is why I was so surprised by the way they reacted to my being gay.

First I needed to know just what they knew.

Back in the living room with my parents, I asked, "What

are you talking about?" This was in response to my mom's question about my being gay. I tried my best to sound confused, yet casual, determined to get to the bottom of this "misunderstanding," but a pit had already opened deep in my stomach.

"A friend of mine said her son said you're a member of the school's gay-straight alliance!" my mom said. She said this pointedly, like she was accusing me of some terrible crime. Which, if you think green shoelaces are an offense against God, I guess it is.

So my mom knew about our gay-straight alliance (technically, a gay-straight-*bisexual* alliance, but I sure wasn't going to correct her!). I know it might sound strange that it had taken a whole eight months for word to get around to her, but it really wasn't. It wasn't just my parents and I who lived on different continents. It was *all* teenagers, and *all* adults. And eight months is about how long it takes for gossip to get from one continent to another, at least without the Internet, which my parents hardly ever used.

"I *am* a member of the gay-straight alliance," I said. "Wouldn't you be? It's a question of civil rights. But that doesn't mean I'm *gay*!" Now I tried to sound shocked at the suggestion, but not, of course, offended.

"Then I went looking in your room," my mom said. "And I found this."

She threw the skull onto the love seat and snatched up something from the coffee table. It was a magazine that Otto had sent me. Not a porno one, mind you. Just a gay teen magazine.

It was so incredibly *wrong* of her to be looking in my room without my permission! If she'd had a question about my sexuality, she could have *asked*. True, I might have evaded the question. I was good at that. (For example, I had just finished saying that being a member of the gay-straight alliance didn't necessarily mean *I* was gay . . . which is technically true!) But I had never lied to my parents before, and I wasn't about to start now.

I took a deep breath. "It's true," I said. "What you said before."

You know how animals look right after the crash of thunder—incredibly alert with the fur on their backs sticking up? That's how I felt. As for my parents' total invasion of my privacy in going through my things, I'd decided to let that go for now.

My parents were momentarily speechless. My mom sank down onto the couch next to a couple of paper gravestones—Halloween decorations still to be put away.

"But Russel!" she said. "Why didn't you *tell* us?"

She was kidding, right?

"You're confused!" my dad said, still hugging the paper coffin. "That's it, isn't it? Lots of kids go through a phase like this. I know I did."

This caught me by surprise. My dad went through a "gay" phase? But I didn't even want to take a single step down that avenue of thought.

"I'm not confused," I said, trying to keep my voice even, confident. "I've known for a long time. Maybe forever."

This was true. Being gay was never that big a deal for me. Maybe it was because I always felt so unbelievably different from other kids in so many other ways anyway—this was just one more thing. What *had* been a big deal was figuring out how I was going to live my whole life without anyone ever finding out. I hadn't counted on the fact that not telling people would make me feel so dishonest, so schizophrenic, and so incredibly lonely. So that previous spring, I had finally decided that maybe I could both be gay *and* tell people about it.

"But you *can't* know!" my mom was saying. "Russel, you're only sixteen years old!"

"Almost seventeen," I said. My birthday was in a month.

I thought about trying to explain—that I *did* know I was gay. That I wasn't going through some phase, that I wasn't

"questioning my sexuality." For me, being gay was just finally finding the word to describe the way I'd always felt. And the word *did* fit, perfectly. I knew I was gay exactly the way I knew I was a boy, or had red hair (more auburn, really).

But I also knew, just as certainly, that my parents couldn't hear this. Not now, anyway.

"Why don't we talk about this later?" I said.

"Russel!" my dad said. "I think you really need to think about this!"

And then my mom said, "But, Russel! Homosexuality is *disgusting*!"

I need to stop here for a second. I know I've been making jokes about this whole little episode. Looking back, it's funny to think how my parents reacted. Ha, ha. But it didn't feel funny at the time. People like to say that we gay people don't know what it's like to experience "real" discrimination—that we were never slaves, that we never had our land stolen from us, that we were never put in concentration camps (wait, yes, we were—okay, bad example). But let me say here and now that being rejected by your own parents just for being yourself is really, really tough. Sure, other minorities have had it bad (like it's some contest!), but at least they grew up in families surrounded by people just like themselves. No matter how bad they had

it, no matter how bad the discrimination is or was, at least most of them had one another.

Meanwhile, most of us gay people grow up surrounded by people who we know don't understand us and who, if they knew the truth, might very well completely reject us. Then when they finally do learn the truth, most of our parents *do* reject us, at least for a little while. And there is nothing—and I mean *nothing!*—like being rejected by your own parents, even if you don't have anything in common with them. These are still the people who raised you, who are supposed to love you unconditionally.

Just something to think about, okay?

Anyway, there I was, and my mom had just said to me, "But, Russel! Homosexuality is *disgusting!*"

In other words, *I* was disgusting.

I just stared at my parents. It was like I suddenly didn't know them. It was like they had both ripped off rubber masks, and I could see their real faces for the first time—faces that were terrifying and evil and lifeless, just like, well, zombies.

I desperately needed to talk to someone. I was all set to IM Min or Gunnar when I noticed an e-mail in my in-box.

An e-mail from Kevin.

I meant what I said. I really need to talk to you, okay?

He needed to talk to me, and I needed to talk to a friend. Kevin was a friend, right? So before I could stop myself, I found myself IMing Kevin and asking if he wanted to meet me at the park between our houses.

We met at this picnic gazebo. It had been built at the edge of a swamp that bordered the park, but since the swamp stank of methane, the picnic gazebo did too. This was the place where we used to meet when we'd been boyfriends, so even though it stunk to high heaven, it was still a romantic place to me. In the months since our ill-fated affair, I'd gotten, um, aroused every time I smelled sulfur.

By this point I was already 90 percent certain that my IMing Kevin had been a mistake. Meeting at the stinky picnic gazebo, with all its history, was just compounding the mistake. But I'd said I was coming, so it would have been rude to just not show up.

He was waiting for me underneath the gazebo.

"Russel!" he said, too loudly. "Thanks for coming!"

"Yeah, well, something just happened. I needed to talk to someone."

"Yeah?"

"My parents just found out I'm gay. They found a magazine."

Now this was very strange. Notice how I didn't tell him who the magazine was from? It was almost like I didn't want him knowing I had a boyfriend. What was *that* about?

"Oh, man!" Kevin said. "What'd they do?"

I told Kevin the whole horrible encounter.

"Gosh, Russel, I'm so sorry!" He sort of shuffled nervously, and I could tell he was thinking about hugging me. But in the end he didn't move any closer, which made me feel relieved and disappointed at the same time. "Are you okay?"

"I don't know," I said. "I guess so. I mean, I think so. My parents can't stay mad forever, right?" I *did* feel better. Talking to Kevin, just saying everything out loud, had helped. "Hey, what did you want to talk to me about anyway?"

"Huh? Oh, you mean my e-mail. Well, it's funny, because it's a little like you. I'm coming out. Well, not to my parents, but to my friends. At school, I mean."

Time screeched to a halt, leaving skid marks in the bottom of my stomach. Kevin was coming out? This was a very big deal.

I shook my head. "I don't believe it," I said. It was kind of a jerky thing to say, but I couldn't help myself.

"No, I am," he said. "Really!"

I peered at him. "When?"

"Soon. I want to tell my buddies on the baseball team first. So they don't hear it from someone else. I know I need to tell them one at a time."

So he'd actually given this some thought. Was he really going to go through with it? I had my doubts.

"Well," I said. "That is some big news. How do you feel?"

He bobbed and weaved. "Scared. But excited too. It just feels right. Anyway, I wanted to tell you right away."

Something about that statement seemed unfinished. Like there was more he wanted to say.

"Wow," I said again. "Well, that's great. And I'm glad you told me."

"So," he said.

"Yeah," I said.

"I knew you'd be surprised."

"I am. I really am."

"But it feels good," Kevin said. "Really, really good."

"Well, I'm happy for you."

Why did it suddenly feel like the conversation had come to a standstill? Now we were just spinning our wheels.

There was something that wasn't being said here—the real reason why Kevin had wanted to tell me he was coming out. It was obvious, right? Or was it? Maybe I was just flattering myself.

The thing is, I didn't *want* to know what was not being said here. I had a boyfriend, right? And I was very happy with him. The fact that Kevin was coming out—*if* he ever actually did—didn't change anything at all. Kevin had been a real jerk to me, and there was no taking that back.

"Well, look," I said. "I should get home. School night and all, right?"

"Russel?" Kevin said.

"Good luck with your friends!" I said, starting to leave. Suddenly the most important thing in the world was getting away from him.

But Kevin wasn't going to let me get away that easily. Before I could get five feet, he spoke the words that had been hanging in the air like levitating water balloons; as he spoke them, they splashed down right on top of me.

"Russel," he whispered. "I still love you. I'm so sorry I hurt you before, and if you'll have me, I wanna get back together again."

CHAPTER THREE

So Kevin wanted to get back together. I guess I'd known this all along. Why else would he have wanted to "talk"? But I had a new boyfriend now, that great guy named Otto, and I really, really loved him. So why hadn't I stopped Kevin from saying his horrible and horribly exciting words?

In my defense, I found the courage to mention Otto at last.

"Kevin," I said. "I'm sorry. I have a new boyfriend."

"You *do*?" Kevin couldn't have looked more surprised if I'd told him I was really a werewolf. What was so damn surprising about my having a new boyfriend? Did he think I was such a loser that I'd never find anyone again? But I couldn't blame Kevin for not being aware of Otto.

He had no way of knowing about him. Otto didn't go to our school, and Kevin and I hadn't talked for eight months.

"His name is Otto," I said. "I met him at summer camp. He's a really great guy."

Note to world: Ex-boyfriends really don't want to hear details about how great a new boyfriend is, especially when they're hearing about him for the very first time.

"Oh," Kevin said.

"He lives almost eight hundred miles away." Now why had I told Kevin *that*? Because it sounded suspiciously like a mixed message.

"Oh?"

"But we're really, really happy," I added quickly— lamely.

"Well," Kevin said. "I'm really happy for you. Really." He hesitated. "I should probably get going. Hey, are you gonna be okay about your parents?"

"Yeah," I said. "I'm much better. Thanks for listening."

"Uh-huh."

And then he was the one walking away from me.

So Kevin wanted to get back together with me, so much so that he was willing to come out at school. Or so he said. It remained to be seen if he would ever actually do it. I had

my doubts, especially now that I'd turned him down flat (more or less). The last time Kevin had had to choose between me and his own popularity, he'd chosen his popularity—to the point where he'd even actually stood there with his jock friends calling me names for being gay. That was a hard thing to forget.

I headed off in the opposite direction from Kevin. But the pit in my stomach, the one that had first opened when I realized my parents knew what they knew, hadn't gone away. If anything, it was even bigger than before.

When I got home that night, I slipped in the back door. I could hear my parents talking in the kitchen, but I some- how managed to creep past them. I felt like the main character in some monster movie, trying to get out of the house before the creatures realize I'm there. Only in my case, I was just trying to get to my bedroom.

Once there, I immediately IMed Otto. I was well aware that he should have been the first person whom I told about my parents. I felt guilty, like I'd cheated on him, which I guess in a way I had.

My user name was "Smuggler" (for no reason I can explain). Otto's was "OttoManEmpire" (because, well, his name is Otto).

Smuggler: Hey you. Big news. My parents found out about me.

OttoManEmpire: No WAY! How?

I explained it all, but I didn't mention that it was the magazine he had sent me, because I didn't want him to feel responsible.

OttoManEmpire: How do you feel? Are you okay?

Kevin had asked me the same question. I had to think about it before I could answer Otto. How *did* I feel? So much had happened in such a short period of time, but none of it made much sense. I felt like a leper examining myself for injuries that I knew were there but that I couldn't quite feel.

Smuggler: I'm not sure it's hit me yet.

OttoManEmpire: Yeah, I felt that way too at first.

He had told his parents in August, a few weeks after he'd got home from summer camp. They had been surprised and concerned, but they hadn't called him disgusting.

Smuggler: What's it like with your parents now?

OttoManEmpire: Okay. I told them, and then they never talked about it again. So things basically went back to normal. It's never come up.

Smuggler: Figures.

OttoManEmpire: What you need now is support. Someone you can talk to in person (and who'll give you a hug!). Min or Gunnar around?

Smuggler: I already talked to one friend.

I felt guilty that I hadn't specified that that "friend" was Kevin. At least I hadn't let him hug me.

OttoManEmpire: That's what helped me. The support of my friends.

Otto hadn't told just his parents he was gay—he'd also told all his friends, and even come out at school. My meeting him that summer had changed his whole life, which was cool, but it made me feel strange too. Responsible.

OttoManEmpire: Do your parents know about me?

Smuggler: No. But they might figure it out. They know you're coming for Thanksgiving.

Otto was coming to visit me over the break the following week. We'd been planning it for a while now. I'd already told him about *Attack of the Soul-Sucking Brain Zombies*, and even picked up a form to mail to him so he could get it signed by his parents and be an extra too, at least for a day or two.

OttoManEmpire: Do you think I should still come visit?
Smuggler: YES! I really really really still want you to come!

I also sent him six "party face" emoticons. And I wasn't lying with my answer. I really *did* want him to come. My parents' learning I was gay and Kevin saying he wanted to get back together had left me all confused and my emotions jumbled. But I wasn't confused about my feelings toward Otto. I still remembered Otto's and my last night together, at camp that summer. We had snuck out onto the lake in a rowboat after dark, and we'd cried and kissed and held each other, and told each other how much we were in love. My feelings for him then had been stronger than any-

thing I'd ever experienced, even stronger than what I'd felt for Kevin all those months ago.

OttoManEmpire: But what will your parents say? Especially if we sleep in the same bedroom.

He sent me a "winking face" emoticon.

Smuggler: Who cares? This is my house too!

This was, of course, a gross oversimplification. But I figured I could deal with all that later.

Smuggler: Otto?
OttoManEmpire: Yeah?
Smuggler: I love you. You know that, right?
OttoManEmpire: Of course. And I love you too.
Smuggler: No! I mean I really, really, really love you!

This was absolutely true. There was nothing that I wanted more than to see Otto again, to spend time floating on the calm, moonlit water in the quiet little rowboat of

our love. I want to kiss him, and rest my head on his chest, and smell his hair, and massage the muscles in the back of his neck. I knew it wouldn't change what had happened with my parents, but for as long as we were together, the world would at least feel right.

But as absolutely true as all this was, in the back of my mind was this nagging little feeling that, even now, I kind of wanted to kiss and rest my head and all the rest with Kevin too.

The next day at school, I told Min and Gunnar all about what had happened with my parents. They were very supportive and said all the right things, just like I knew they would.

I didn't tell them about Kevin. Which felt weird. It was like I'd spent all day lifting weights with my right arm, but not my left. I felt out of balance.

Why didn't I tell Min? Partly it was because I knew exactly how she would react. She would say go tell Kevin to take a flying leap. And she would have a point. Kevin had treated me pretty badly all those months before. Min also had her own issues with Kevin. She'd wanted him to stand up for this kid that everyone was bullying, but he never had.

Anyway, this new situation was more complicated than how Min would see it. She was great, but she could be kind

of, um, uncompromising. This is not necessarily a bad thing. She was the kind of friend who calls you on your crap. Everyone should have a friend like her.

But that's not where I was right then. I was still working things through in my mind. Meanwhile, I knew that Gunnar wouldn't judge me. He'd made mistakes too. He was more human. So he just seemed like the better friend to talk to—safer.

On nonrainy days, Gunnar and I rode to school together on our bikes. I decided to tell him about Kevin on the way home.

"It's really incredible the number of big directors who got their start on horror movies," Gunnar was saying as we rode. "James Cameron, Peter Jackson, Sam Raimi, Francis Ford Coppola, Oliver Stone. Even Steven Spielberg!" Needless to say, Gunnar was still obsessing over the making of movies.

"Oh," I said.

"But it's not surprising. Horror really lends itself to low-budget filmmaking. The stories are pretty straightforward, and a lot of what makes a film scary is the camera work, and what's implied on-screen, not what's actually shown. Audiences are also more forgiving of technical flaws, at least if the film is scary. Plus horror is one of the few genres where you can get a distribution deal and promote the movie even with no stars."

"Ah," I said.

Gunnar looked over at me. "Sorry. I'm going on, aren't I? You're still freaked about your parents, aren't you?"

Gunnar acted like he had OCD *and* ADD, but that didn't mean he was completely clueless. He might not have been as observant as I was, but he did okay in a pinch.

"It's not that," I said.

"Then what?"

I sighed. "Kevin."

"Kevin Land? What does he have to do with anything?"

"He wants to get back together."

"You are *kidding* me!"

"No." I explained how I'd run into him at the movie meeting, how he'd e-mailed me afterward, and how we'd met by the stinky picnic gazebo.

"That must be kind of flattering," Gunnar said. "To have him coming crawling back to you and everything."

I laughed. "Yeah. I guess it is. But it's not just that. Kevin told me he's decided to come out."

Gunnar knew why I'd broken up with Kevin, so he knew exactly what this meant.

"Yikes," he said. "Do you think he really will?"

"He might. What do you think I should do?"

"About Kevin?"

"Yeah."

He stared at me for a second. "You're really asking my opinion?"

"Of course," I said. "Why not?"

"Well, it's just that no one's ever really asked me for relationship advice before. Why would they? What do *I* know about relationships?"

"Well, you *do* have a girlfriend now, you know."

"I know! Sometimes I still can't believe it." Gunnar thought a second longer. "If Kevin did come out, would you want to get back together with him?"

That was the million-dollar question. Gunnar had zeroed right in on it. Maybe I'd been wrong not to ask him relationship advice earlier.

"I don't know," I admitted.

"So it's kind of a possibility?" Gunnar asked.

"Maybe."

We kept riding. Our bikes squeaked. My balls needed readjusting, but I couldn't do it without losing my balance.

"What about Otto?" he said at last. There was no judgment in his voice, just like I'd thought.

"God, I love Otto. I really do. No doubt about that."

"But?"

"But he lives eight hundred miles away!" I said. "And I'm almost seventeen years old. If he were here, there would be no question that I would stay with him. But what kind of relationship can we have living that far apart? I'll see him a week or two every year, at most. That's not a relationship, it's a pen pal. And we *can* stay friends. And maybe someday we'll live closer together, so we can pursue a real relationship. There's nothing to keep that from happening. This thing with Kevin, it's not really about Kevin. It's about me. About where I am in life."

"But?"

"But I do love Otto. And Otto loves me. And meeting me, it's changed his whole life. If I broke up with him, he would be devastated. I'm sure he'd think it was his entire fault. It might be forever until he trusted someone again. And why would I really be breaking up with him? Just because there's someone who lives *closer*? What kind of crappy reason is *that*? Maybe I'm just making excuses so I can get back together with Kevin."

"But?"

"But I can't stay with someone out of guilt or obligation. I'd just end up resenting him in the long run, and that's not doing anyone any favors. And if I'm making excuses to get together with Kevin, maybe that's because I *want* to get together with Kevin."

Gunnar fell silent. Sometimes—very rarely, but sometimes—he knew when to stop talking.

"Maybe you'll see things more clearly when Otto visits next week," Gunnar said at last.

"This is true," I said.

"And Kevin might not come out at all. He said he would, but who knows if he will? If he doesn't, you don't have a problem. You don't have to choose."

"I know," I said. I'd already thought about this. In fact, I put the odds of Kevin actually coming out at less than fifty-fifty.

"But if he does?" Gunnar said. "What are you going to do? Who are you going to pick?"

"Gunnar," I said, "if this were a book, I just might skip ahead to the end. Because right now, I have absolutely no idea."

That afternoon after school, I tried doing the sneak-in-the-back-door thing again, but my parents were once again waiting for me in the living room. My dad got home from work at sixty-forty every night. I had never known him to come home early, not even when our washing machine overflowed. So I knew this was a very big deal.

Great, I thought. This was *just* what I needed.

"What," I said. Notice there is no question mark.

"Russel," my dad said. "We need to talk."

They needed to talk? Well, I sure hoped they were going to start by apologizing for calling me disgusting! Even so, I wasn't going to sit down on the love seat across from them. For one thing, I felt no love whatsoever. So if they wanted to talk, I would do it standing up.

"We want to understand," my dad said. "This is hard for us. It's a shock."

I guess this made sense. I'd had my whole life to get used to the idea. They'd barely had twenty-four hours.

I stared at my parents, trying to figure out what to say. I couldn't help but notice that there was dirt under my mom's fingernails. She'd probably been out back fiddling with her bonsai trees—her way to work out stress.

"This is just who I am," I said at last. "I know it's upsetting to you. But most of what you hear about gay people, the stereotypes you see on television, that isn't true. Most of us are just normal people."

"Homosexuality is a sin," my mom said.

Oh, so now I was a sinner too? This was their idea of "talking," of trying to understand? By calling me a sinner?

"Russel," my dad said, "we know that adolescence is a very confusing time."

Yes, I thought to myself. And my dad had gone through a "gay" phase. We'd covered this yesterday.

"I'm not confused," I said. "I'm really not. I know this is new for you, but it's not for me. I've thought about it a lot. I know what I feel. I've known for years." I'd said all this to them once before, but maybe they needed to hear it twice.

"We still think you should talk to someone," my dad said.

"What?" I said. "Why?"

"Because homosexuality is a *sin*!" my mom shouted.

"To help you sort out your feelings," my dad quickly interjected. "To help you make sense of it."

Apparently when my parents said "talk," they meant they wanted to talk *to* me, but not listen to a single word I said in response. Did they really think that would work? If so, well, in a nutshell, they were nuts.

"I told you before," I said. "My feelings don't need sorting out!" Well, okay, maybe they did, but about Kevin and Otto, and how to deal with my parents not listening to me. But not about being gay.

"Just talk to him," my dad said. "Is that too much to ask?"

"Who?" I said.

"Father Franklin."

"Our priest?" My family was Catholic. We went to mass every Sunday. But to tell the truth, the whole "religion" thing had never really worked for me. I considered myself spiritual, and hopefully somewhat moral. But being moral because someone gives you a list of rules to follow (and warns you you'll be punished if you don't), well, that always seemed to me to kind of miss the point. And how can anyone honestly believe that their religion is the "right" one when 99 percent of people just adopt the religion of their parents? But I knew the Catholic thing was important to my parents, so I had always played along.

Still, I wondered where all this talk of sinning and religion was coming from all of a sudden. My parents hadn't mentioned any of this when they'd first found out about me. Then they'd just been worried about what people would think. It's like they were upset because of the way it made them feel, but now they were retroactively applying religion to it, to justify their preexisting feelings.

I'm not saying my parents were hypocrites. I'm just putting it out there, okay?

"Russel, you *can't* be gay!" my mom said, erupting again with a regularity that was suddenly not unlike Old Faithful. "What would our friends say?"

I give up: it's true, my parents *were* hypocrites.

"He'll *help* you," my dad interjected. "Father Franklin? He's good at this kind of thing."

"I don't need help," I repeated. "You guys sound like you're the ones who need the help. Why don't *you* talk to Father Franklin?"

"We can all talk to him together if you'd like."

That was all I needed. Three against one!

"No, that's okay," I said.

"So you'll talk to him?" my dad asked me.

At that point, it seemed like there was only one thing I could say to get my parents to shut up. Besides, they were my parents. What could I do?

"Yeah," I said. "I'll talk to the damn priest."

CHAPTER FOUR

THAT SATURDAY, WE HAD our first day of extra work on *Attack of the Soul-Sucking Brain Zombies*. We had a wardrobe-and-makeup call at eight in the morning, so Gunnar and Em picked me up at seven-thirty. Min wasn't with us—she had her own car and lived on the opposite side of town anyway.

I felt like crap on a cracker. I am so not a morning person.

As we drove to the shoot, Gunnar enlightened us on another aspect of moviemaking.

"That board they knock together before every scene?" he said. "That's called a clapper board. They use it to keep track of each take in postproduction. They record the sound and the film image on two different machines, you know? So they need some way to make sure that the image matches up with the right sound track."

"I thought they rerecorded all the dialogue anyway," Em said.

"Not always," he said. "Sometimes they try to keep the on-set dialogue, because it looks and sounds more natural."

We drove into the school parking lot, and I spotted Min and Kevin over by his car. It looked like they were talking. I wondered what they were talking *about*.

We pulled up next to them, and I climbed out of the car.

"Hey," I said.

"Morning!" Kevin said.

Min just rolled her eyes. I wasn't sure what that was about. Had they been talking about me?

We walked toward the school as a group.

"Why do we need makeup anyway?" Kevin said, a little too loudly. "They're not turning us into zombies yet. Aren't we just normal teenagers today?"

"It's so our faces don't shine in the movie lights," Gunnar said. "It won't be full makeup."

"Well, what about wardrobe?" Kevin said. "Don't we already dress like normal teenagers? We *are* normal teenagers."

Even Gunnar didn't have an answer for that one.

Soon I found myself walking side by side with Kevin. "Isn't it funny?" he said, talking too loudly again. "We get

up this early every morning. But today it seems *early*. Is it just because it's Saturday?"

"Probably," I said. But to myself, I was wondering why I hadn't ever noticed before how Kevin's voice got louder when he got nervous. What exactly was he nervous *about*?

Just inside the school, there were a couple of production assistants waiting for us at a table. They took our parental release forms (I had told my dad it was "a school project," which it sort of was). Then they gave us each a plastic number, and said they'd call when it was our turn to be made pretty. I was number two.

Finally, a production assistant led us to the school cafeteria, which she referred to as the "hospitality suite." There was only one other person waiting inside, a girl.

Min immediately dropped her plastic number.

I bent down to pick it up for her. "Oops," I said, giving it back. "You dropped this."

She didn't answer.

The producers had set out some food—doughnuts, bagels, fruit, and juice—on one of the cafeteria tables. Min headed over to check it out. Maybe it was early morning hunger that was distracting her.

Meanwhile, Gunnar was still talking. "I bet they storyboarded this whole movie," he said. "That's when they illustrate the film, like in a giant comic book. They show all the

angles, and how the camera is going to move. It's especially important on a film like this one, one with lots of action."

"I made a comic book once," Kevin said. "In the sixth grade. Problem was, my teacher wanted it to be about Jamestown, and I wanted it to be about Batman."

"Sometimes they storyboard the whole movie," Gunnar was saying. "And sometimes they only do it for the action scenes. It depends on the director."

"I did the whole story of Jamestown," Kevin said. "But if you look in the background in some of the panels, you can see Batman in the distance."

My head throbbed. It was only eight fifteen in the morning, but between Kevin's nervous prattle and Gunnar's ongoing film seminar, I was almost ready to call it a day.

It was true what they say about making movies: it's mostly just a lot of sitting around. But for a newbie like me, just watching them arrange the lights and position the cameras was interesting.

For Gunnar, meanwhile, it was like a spaceship had descended from the sky in the shape of a gigantic electric birthday cake, and aliens had emerged in the form of naked women with enormous breasts.

They had made us extras up as members of various high

school cliques (which is why we couldn't just wear our own clothes). They'd dressed Gunnar and me as computer nerds, and Kevin as a jock—both arguably decent casting choices. They'd also given us all green socks. I wondered what the socks were about, but being a lowly extra, mine was not to question why. . . .

As for the girls, they'd pegged Em as a goth girl and Min as a cheerleader. (And for the record, just seeing Min dressed up as a cheerleader made this whole moviemaking experience worthwhile, no matter what happened next. She looked completely stunned by her costume assignment, like a cat who'd just fallen into the bathtub!)

According to Gunnar, the scenes of most movies are not shot in the order in which you watch them. But in our case, the first scene they shot really was one of the very first scenes in the movie. It was the scene where the main character, a new kid in a small town, comes to his new high school for the first time.

We extras were just supposed to mill around in the hallway, acting like members of our various cliques. Meanwhile, to play the jocks and cheerleaders in the foreground, the ones with speaking parts, the producers had hired real actors (who, incidentally, looked nothing whatsoever like real high school students; I doubt any of them were under the age of twenty-five or had even a single zit).

The production assistants got everything set up for the scene, with all the extras and "real" actors in place.

Then the star of the movie walked onto the set.

Declan McDonnell.

Yes, *that* Declan McDonnell! The one who played the womanizing best friend of the star of that big sitcom a few years back? He'd also done a few movies, but nothing breakout.

He was *totally* dreamy. He had straight black hair that he parted in the middle, a crooked smile, and blue-green eyes that were supposedly the color of the ocean. (Full disclosure: I had a picture of him, shirtless, in My Pictures.)

I desperately wanted to meet him. Thing is, I knew that could never happen, even if he wasn't an internationally famous movie star and I wasn't a complete nobody. After all, they had specifically told us that we couldn't talk to the stars.

I pulled Gunnar aside. "That's Declan McDonnell!" I said breathlessly.

"Who?" he said.

It figured he would know nothing about movies that had anything to do with actual human beings.

"He's famous," I said, deliberately dialing it down. "He's been in movies."

"Oh," Gunnar said. "Huh."

Right then, the director called "Rolling!", which meant that we extras were supposed to start doing our "extra" thing, acting like high school students. The "jocks" started strutting around like jocks, the "cheerleaders" twirled and flitted like cheerleaders, and the "nerds" like Gunnar and me crept back and forth like antisocial computer nerds.

The director called "Action!", which meant the real actors were supposed to start acting.

Out of the corner of my eye, I watched the scene in the foreground unfold. Declan McDonnell entered through the front doors. The "real" jocks and cheerleaders, the ones played by actors, all laughed at him for wearing white socks, not green ones.

A few minutes later, the director yelled, "Cut!"

Then we had to do it all over again.

But this time, one of the "extra" jocks, probably taking a cue from what was going on in the foreground, decided it would be more realistic if he started picking on the nerds—namely, Gunnar and me.

He deliberately bumped up against me in the hall-way—roughly, I might add. "Outta my way, nerd!" he said.

Kevin, who was standing with him, hesitated a second. Then he added, "Yeah, outta our way, nerds."

I couldn't help but remember the time that Kevin had

done almost this exact same thing to me for real, joining in with his jock friends and teasing me, not because I was a nerd, but because I was gay. I'd learned then what was obviously still true now: Kevin just did what those around him did. Despite his muscles, he was fundamentally weak.

"Good!" the director called to us. "Jock extras? Keep teasing the nerds! That's perfect!"

After the first couple of takes, the camera jammed (or something), and we were told it would be a few minutes before filming resumed.

Kevin immediately stepped up next to me. "Can you believe that's really *Declan McDonnell*?" he said, as breathless as I had been before. "Damn, he's hot!"

Of course it took another gay boy to see the obviousness of such things. But I wasn't breathless anymore. I was irritated that Kevin had been so quick to tease me just because someone else had first. Frankly, I was annoyed that Kevin was even at this movie shoot at all.

I turned to face him. "Kevin, why are you doing this?"

"What?" he said. "You mean the teasing? Sorry about that. But it's what the director wanted."

Yeah, I wanted to point out, but you started teasing us *before* the director had said he liked it!

"It's not about the teasing," I said, because it mostly wasn't. "Why are you here at all? This isn't your thing.

You're a jock—for real, I mean. You should be out doing jumping jacks somewhere."

"Whaddaya mean? I wanted to be in a movie."

"Admit it, Kevin. You're here because of me."

"That's not true!" But I could tell I was right because he was suddenly talking louder than before.

"Kevin," I said. "I'm really flattered that you want to get back together with me, but it can't work. I have a boyfriend. So that's that. We're not getting back together, okay?"

There, I thought. I had nipped this thing in the bud. I'd stopped him in his tracks and cut him off at the pass. How much clearer could I be?

"Sure," he said. The weird thing is, suddenly he wasn't talking loudly anymore. And then he flashed me a grin that was even more impish than usual.

Sunday night was when I had to go see Father Franklin— specifically, to the rectory, which is what they call the place where the priest lives. His housekeeper met me and led me to his office, where he was working at his desk. Father Franklin was an old man with a rotund body and a boyish face. Imagine a gigantic baby, and you won't be far off.

His office smelled like incense—but not just any incense. The funeral kind, thick and serious. It made the whole office smell like a crypt.

He stood up when he saw me. He was dressed all in black with the white collar and everything. "Russel!" he said. "Come in, come in! It's good to see you again."

"Ah," I said. It *wasn't* good to see him again, and I wasn't going to lie and say it was.

We shook hands, which still made me feel like an idiot whenever I did it with an adult.

"Your parents said we should talk," he said.

"Yeah, they did," I said.

By now, the housekeeper had left, but she hadn't closed the door behind us. Neither did Father Franklin. My first thought was, Is this church policy? Could priests no longer be alone with teenage boys? But then I felt bad for thinking this. How tough would it be to have the whole world wondering if you're a child molester?

"Have a seat!" Father Franklin said. "Have a seat."

I sat in the leather chair across from his desk.

"I can't believe how you've grown," he said. "Seems like just last week you were a boy."

This, of course, is just what every teenager loves to hear.

"So." The priest cleared his throat. "Your parents said you're having some questions about your sexuality."

I shook my head. "No, I don't have any questions. I've known that I'm gay for a long time. But my parents just found out about it, so they sent me here."

"I see." Father Franklin looked thoughtful. "Why do you think you're gay?"

"Why does anyone think they're anything? I just do."

Father Franklin nodded. "Right. But Russel, adolescence is a very confusing time. I'm sure I don't need to tell you that. It's common for boys to go through different phases."

Oh, God, not Father Franklin too. Had every adult gone through a "gay" phase? Or were they just telling me this so I'd think they had some "street cred" on the issue?

"I'm not confused," I said. "This is actually one of the things in my life that I'm least confused about. That and the fact that there are too many superhero movies."

Father Franklin stared at me.

"That was a joke," I said.

He completely ignored my attempt at humor, which kind of sucked. "Russel, your parents are just concerned about you. Once you go public with something like this, there can be real consequences."

"All my friends already know," I said. "My whole school knows. I started a gay-straight-bisexual alliance. My parents were the last to know. And there *were* consequences. But the way I see it, the only way things are ever going to change is if people take a stand for what they believe. I actually think that's kind of the moral thing to do. Don't you?"

Father Franklin shifted in his seat. I was making him nervous. I hate to admit it, but I was enjoying this.

"Well, you may be right," he went on. I think he knew he needed to try a different approach. "You probably think that the Catholic Church doesn't have any guidance to offer someone in a situation like yours."

That was *exactly* what I thought. But I didn't say it out loud.

"But the Catholic Church is two thousand years old," he said. "It's lasted that long for a reason. I'm not saying the church hasn't made mistakes. It has. But I believe that the reason it's lasted as long as it has is because it's been charged with certain unchanging truths."

"Like what?" I said.

"Like on the subject of human sexuality. That sex is a gift from God. But one that comes with certain responsibilities. We can't just go around having sex with whoever we want. Actions have consequences. That's the basis for all morality."

"I totally agree with that," I said. "Sex is a big deal. Most people take it way too lightly."

Father Franklin smiled and sat up in his seat. He was relieved. He had found common ground with me at last.

"God gave us sex," the priest said, "but he put limits on it too. First and foremost, he asks that we save sex for the sacrament of marriage."

Here we go, I thought to myself. At the same time, it seemed like the incense was growing thicker. Sickly sweet too. Suddenly I could hardly breathe.

"But gay people can't get married," I said. "Where does that leave us?"

He coughed quietly. "Well, gay people have a special calling from God. The Church teaches that God calls gay people to be celibate. That means to refrain from sexual activity."

I knew what it meant. Yes, that was a "special" calling, wasn't it? Sort of like God calling houseflies to eat dog crap.

I didn't say anything, so there was a silence. The purring of the electric clock sounded like someone clearing his throat, but in a way that never made it any better.

"Why?" I said at last.

"What?" Father Franklin said.

"I'm sorry, but that just doesn't make any sense to me. Why would God treat gay and straight people so differently? It's not fair."

"I know it seems that way. But God places limits on heterosexual people too."

"Yes," I said, "but if straight people don't agree to those limits, you'll marry them anyway. And most Catholics *don't* agree with those limits." I knew this for a fact. I was no fool. Before coming here, I'd done my research.

Father Franklin was back to shifting in his seat. "Russel,

I'm not just making these things up, you know. There are traditions. These things come directly from Scripture."

"There used to be a tradition to keep slaves," I said. "The Church used to say that came from Scripture too, until they decided they were wrong. Maybe you're wrong about this too. Back when the Bible was being written, no one had any idea what homosexuality was, just like they had no idea that the earth revolved around the sun."

Father Franklin held up his hand. "I'm sorry, Russel, but sex between two men just isn't a part of God's plan!"

This annoyed me. "Who said anything about sex?" I said. "I never told you I was having sex. I never brought up sex at all. You did, twice now. I'm talking about love. And it seems weird to me that the Church would say that two people falling in love is, like, this big, horrible thing, all against God's plan. I just can't believe God would demand that all these people be miserable and alone their whole lives. Or that they marry someone they can't ever really love."

To his credit, Father Franklin just listened. I think he knew I had a point. The air seemed to have cleared a little too. I think the housekeeper had opened a window somewhere.

Father Franklin leaned forward in his chair. "Russel, I can tell you're very smart. So can I be frank?"

"Yes," I said. "Be frank."

"I know that human sexuality is a little more complicated

than the Church sometimes admits in public. When it comes to sex, things aren't always black and white."

Here we go, I thought. Back to sex again. And they say we gay people are obsessed with it?

"What do you mean?" I asked.

"Well, I wasn't born yesterday."

I thought, Oh, God, now I have to hear about Father Franklin's "gay" phase again!

"Yeah?" I said.

"I know the Church can seem uncompromising," the priest said. "And out of touch. But the Church also says that ultimately we have to decide these things for ourselves. That they're a matter of personal conscience."

"So you're saying that if I disagree with you, that's okay?"

"I'm saying that none of this means there isn't still a place for you in the Catholic Church."

Okay, so now I was thoroughly confused. What happened to Unchanging Truths? God's plan? And why hadn't he mentioned this right when I came in? Why did he bring it up only when he realized that I wasn't an intellectual pushover? Were the truths unchanging only for stupid people?

"If the world isn't black and white," I said, "why does the Church talk like it is?"

He thought for a second. "I think some people in the Church think that if we admit we could be wrong about

any one thing, then some people will think we're wrong about *everything*. One of the things that people really like about the Catholic Church is the idea that it's solid. Ageless. Something to cling to in times of change."

"So your stand on gays is really more of a PR decision?" I said.

Father Franklin looked at me. Then he laughed out loud. This time, I hadn't meant to be telling a joke.

"Father Franklin," I said, "now can I be frank with you?"

He looked surprised, like a baby who had just touched a hot lightbulb. "Of course."

"The Church teaches things," I said. "People like my parents hear those things, and they believe them. And then they freak out when they learn their son is gay. And other people hear those things, and they beat up gay people. Or they vote for politicians who write laws that make us second-class citizens. And now you're telling me that the things the Church teaches might not be right after all?"

"What's your point?"

"Actions have consequences, Father. That's the basis for all morality."

"Ah, yes," Father Franklin said. "I see what you mean. Touché."

I stood up. "I'm going to be leaving now. Is that okay, Father?"

"Huh? Oh, yes. Of course." He stood up too. "You probably don't want to hear this, but the Church could use more people like you. I hope you'll still give us a chance."

"Well," I said. "Let's just say I wouldn't wait by the phone."

Needless to say, the air outside the building was fresh and clean.

The next day at school, Monday, Min met me in the hallway.

"Hey!" I said.

She asked how it was going with my parents, and I told her. I felt guilty I hadn't kept her up-to-date on everything that was going on with Kevin. She was one of my best friends. And if she called me on my crap, well, maybe I needed my crap called on right then.

"Here's the thing," she said. "I have a confession to make. It was an accident, but I still feel really bad."

"Yeah?" I said. "I've got something I want to tell you too." I *would* tell her—everything.

But before Min could say anything more, a voice stopped us both dead in our tracks.

"Did you hear?" someone said. "Kevin Land came out! He's *gay!*"

CHAPTER FIVE

So Kevin Land really had come out of the closet.

Wow, I thought, standing in the hallway with Min. Good for him.

Good for him, but bad for me. Because as long as he was in the closet, I didn't have to choose between him and Otto. Now I did. He'd also proven that maybe he wasn't quite as weak as I'd thought. All this was what he'd been impishly grinning about on the movie set on Saturday. He knew by coming out, he would change everything.

Suddenly I wasn't so sure I wanted Min calling me on my crap.

Otto IMed me that night.

OttoManEmpire: Hey, you! How's it going with your parents?

I told him about my encounter with Father Franklin the day before.

OttoManEmpire: Oh man! I wish I could have heard that!
Smuggler: It was oddly satisfying. What's going on with you?

He told me how he and his friends Jan and Will were doing volunteer work at a "no-kill" animal shelter. It was interesting, but to be honest, I didn't know any of the people he was talking about. So it wasn't that interesting.

There was a pause. Neither of us typed anything. It probably wasn't that long of a pause, but it seemed long. I guess it was symbolic or whatever.

OttoManEmpire: Oh! I forgot to ask. Have you reminded your parents that I'm coming for a visit since they found out about you? I'd hate to get all the way there, and then have them send me back home again.

Otto was right. I really didn't know how my parents would react to my having my boyfriend visit, even if they didn't know he was my boyfriend. It wasn't fair to put Otto in such an uncomfortable position.

I needed to talk to my parents again.

My mom was in the kitchen making dinner. It wasn't until she noticed me in the doorway that she started banging the pots and pans.

"What?" I said.

She slammed a cookie sheet onto the counter. "Russel, you could have at least *talked* to the man!"

"Who?"

"Father Franklin!"

"I *did* talk to him!" I said. "I went to see him at his office, just like you said."

"Oh, I heard about that little office visit! He said there wasn't anything he could do to help you if you didn't want help!"

So my mom and Father Franklin had been in contact. I'm not sure why I was surprised.

"It sounds like you didn't just want me to talk to him," I said. "It sounds like you wanted me to let him talk me out of being gay."

"Russel, that's not it at all." But from the way she bumped against the fruit basket, I knew I was right.

"Look," I said. "I wanted to remind you that my friend Otto is coming for Thanksgiving. Remember, my friend from camp?"

"Yes, I know," my mom said quickly. "Wednesday through Saturday."

"Okay," I said, and suddenly I couldn't get out of that kitchen fast enough.

"Wait," my mom said.

Against my wishes, I turned to look at her. It was like I could actually see the activity inside her head, the wheels turning and clicking into place.

"This Otto, he's more than just a friend, isn't he?" she said. Her eyes looked up at mine, boring into them like titanium drill bits.

My parents were nothing like me, true, but they definitely weren't stupid.

Now I had a choice. I could tell the truth and have to deal with their inevitable wrath, and also maybe screw up any chance I had of their letting Otto come visit. Or I could lie, and potentially avoid the whole issue, but risk having them be even more furious if they found out I was lying— and possibly take their fury out on Otto once he arrived.

"Maybe," I said to my mom. Once again, it didn't seem fair to make Otto have to deal with something that was my responsibility. Besides, like I said before, I didn't lie to my parents. I was a good kid. You might even say a *sickeningly* good kid (my classmates had said that often enough). I didn't drink or swear or take drugs or lie to my parents, except for the being-in-the-closet thing, which obviously doesn't count. This is part of the reason why their whole disapproving-of-me-for-being-gay thing was so upsetting. It was like my being gay completely overwhelmed everything else about me.

"*Maybe?*" my mom said to me, meaning my answer to the question about Otto being my boyfriend.

"Okay, yeah, he is," I said. "But it's not like it sounds. You're just hearing the word *boyfriend*. He's a really great guy!"

"*You have a boyfriend?*" Those wheels that I'd seen turning in her head? The whole cuckoo clock was suddenly exploding, with springs and gears blasting everywhere. "Russel, that is *completely* out of the question! I absolutely *forbid* you to have anything to do with this boy!"

Okay, this was not going well. I'm not sure what I was expecting—my parents to take out a same-sex wedding announcement in the local newspaper? But it never

occurred to me that Having a Boyfriend would be as upsetting to them as Being Gay. I mean, weren't they basically the same thing? In retrospect, I saw just how naive I had been.

"Wait! Stop!" I said. "You haven't even met him yet! Just wait till you meet him, okay? He's a really, really, *really* great guy!"

My mom stared at me with this bewildered look, like she didn't recognize me—like I was someone who had just wandered in off the street, someone she'd never even seen before.

Fair enough, I guess. Because I'm sure the look on my face as I stared back at her was one she'd never seen anywhere before.

That Saturday we had another full day of shooting, which meant another 8 A.M. makeup call. Apparently the student body had already started its gradual transformation into zombies, because the makeup artists gave all our faces a yellow tint. They also put dark circles under our eyes and messed up our hair, which they then locked into place with hairspray. (Who knew zombies were so glam?)

Once we were all gathered in the hospitality suite, they said they were going to divide us into two groups, each one working on a different set of scenes.

"That'll be first and second unit," said Gunnar to Min, Em, and me.

"What?" Min said, sounding panicky for some reason.

"Second unit is when they shoot shots that don't include the main characters," Gunnar explained. "Like exterior, identifying shots. Or background shots for special effects. It's called 'second unit' because the director doesn't need to be there, just the second unit director, who's usually a nobody. They'll probably use half of us for the second unit work, and half of us for work with the real director and the stars."

I didn't really care what "first and second unit" meant, but I didn't want to end up in Kevin's group. I guess it's like what they say about alcoholics: if there's booze around, they'll drink it. Kevin was my alcohol, but I didn't want to drink him (okay, that came out really, really wrong).

Needless to say, Kevin and I ended up in the same group. I saw his eyes scanning for me like the sweep of a lighthouse.

I ignored him and hurried over to a production assistant.

"Um," I said to her, "would it be possible to switch units?"

"Sorry," she said. "We need exact numbers."

"How about if I switch with someone?" I pointed to Min, who had been chosen for the other group. "She's my

friend. I'm sure she'll switch with me."

"Why do you want to switch?" the production assistant asked me.

I had to think fast. "I'm epileptic," I lied. "But it's okay because my other friend Gunnar knows how to administer my medicine. Thing is, he's in that group." I pointed to the Kevin-free group, the one I wanted to be in.

Her face immediately shifted to sympathy. "Sure, sure, that's fine."

Next I pulled Min aside. "Do you mind if we switch groups?" I asked.

"What?" she said. "*Why?*" She looked put out, which confused me.

I leaned in closer. "I'm trying to avoid Kevin."

"I don't think that's okay with the producers," she said. "Switching, I mean."

"No, it's okay," I said. "I just asked."

"But—" Min said.

"What?" I said.

She thought for a second—about what, I had no idea. What difference did it make what group she was in?

But finally, she said, "Well, then. Okay."

Tragedy averted, I thought—for a few hours at least.

* * *

Halfway through the morning, they gave us a break, and we all headed back to the hospitality suite. But I wanted to explore the school a bit (and I needed to use the restroom), so I veered off on my own.

It was an older school, churchlike, with echoing hallways and a polished stone floor. But it had been "updated" in the sixties, slathered with industrial green paint and given a horrible white cork ceiling, which was now yellow with water stains. It desperately needed the renovation that was taking place beyond the sheets of milky plastic that draped down over so many of the hallways.

It also needed more bathrooms. It took me forever to find one. But finally I did, a cavernous concrete chamber at the bottom of a small flight of steps (apparently in the previous century, disabled people didn't need restrooms). The wall to my left was nothing but a long row of white porcelain urinals—the tall kind that go all the way down to the floor, so that you can't miss, no matter how lousy your aim. There had to be thirty urinals in all. I couldn't help but wonder if they'd ever all been used at the same time.

As I stepped toward the urinals, I caught sight of someone over to my right, by the long row of porcelain sinks.

It was Declan McDonnell, the star of *Attack of the Soul-*

Sucking Brain Zombies. He'd been washing his hands. My first thought was, What if I'd come in two minutes earlier? Would I have had to pee next to Declan McDonnell? At least with thirty urinals, I could have put a whole bunch of them between the two of us.

"Oh," he said, turning, surprised to see me. "Hello."

I started to say something, but then I remembered how they'd warned us not to talk to the stars. Could I talk to him now that he'd talked to me? The producer hadn't said anything about that.

"Uh," I said at last. "Hi."

"Something wrong?" Declan McDonnell said.

I grimaced. "It's just that they . . ."

"Ah, right. You're not supposed to talk to the stars. The first movie I did, I didn't know that they always tell the crew and the extras that. I just thought everyone was being stuck up." Declan McDonnell's voice rang in the soaring cathedral that was this particular men's room.

But right then, I noticed that Declan McDonnell had forgotten to zip his zipper. (It is *not* that I was looking at his crotch! It's just that I'm observant, remember? His underwear was black, if you must know.)

"Um," I said. "You . . ." I nodded at his crotch but was careful not to stare.

"Huh?" he said. He looked down. "Oh! Thanks! Sorry."

He zipped up.

Seeing Declan McDonnell up close was strange. I'd never seen any face so perfect. It was nice, but it was also a little off-putting. It was like being in the presence of an angel (despite the previously unzipped fly).

"Don't you have your own bathrooms?" I asked.

He shrugged. "Yeah. Sometimes I just need to get away. But I should get back to the set."

"Right," I said. I nodded to the urinals. "And I should, well, pee. Hey, do you think you. . . ?"

But when I turned back to look at him, he was gone, just like an angel having flown right back up to heaven.

I left that bathroom in a daze. It all seemed so unreal. I had actually talked to Declan McDonnell!

I spent the rest of the day avoiding Kevin and, yes, looking for Declan again. It was a disorienting experience, made even worse by the fact that I never did see Declan, but I kept spotting Kevin everywhere I turned.

We worked until six that night. It was a long day, but it's not like I particularly wanted to go home to parents who thought I was "disgusting." I wasn't even annoyed when Gunnar and Em wanted to stay late to watch the cinematographer clean the camera lens.

I went out to wait for them in the parking lot. It was

already dark, which meant I'd spent the whole day indoors, but it was somehow comforting too, like the whole world had pulled up the covers. The fresh air was nice, especially after so much time inside.

The hood of one of the cars in the parking lot was standing open. Somehow I knew exactly who I'd find under that hood.

Sure enough, Kevin poked his head out.

"Russel!" he said, smiling.

"Kevin," I said. It was too late now to pretend I hadn't seen him, so I walked closer.

"Dead battery," he said, nodding to his car. "Left my lights on this morning."

"That sucks. You have jumper cables?"

He nodded and held up two ends, one red and one black.

"You know how to hook them up?" I asked.

"Oh, sure," he said. This figured. Kevin was just that butch.

"Gunnar'll be out in a sec," I said. "I'm sure he'll give you a jump."

"Yeah, I was waiting for you guys." We stood there for a minute, not talking, sort of facing in different directions. Then Kevin said, "So I guess you heard about me, huh?"

Kevin meant about his coming out. And of course I'd

heard. It was all anyone had been talking about all week.

"Yeah," I said. "That's really great. Congratulations."

"You didn't think I'd really do it, did you?" He sounded a little proud, which was okay, because he'd done something to be proud of.

"No," I admitted. "I guess not." But I didn't want to talk about this. After all, I'd told him before that the reason we couldn't be together was because I was out and he wasn't. Now that had changed.

"It's hard though," Kevin said. "People can sure be assholes. Thing like this shows you who your friends really are."

It was only then that I noticed that Kevin had a black eye. The skin under his eye was a purple wash even in the wan overhead light of that parking lot. At first I thought it might be makeup from the shoot, but it looked far too real.

Kevin had been in a fight with someone, no doubt over his coming out. I wondered who. One of the other jocks? His dad?

Suddenly I wanted to comfort him with a hug. He wasn't my boyfriend anymore, but he was still a friend. And didn't friends hug each other when one of them was in pain? I didn't want to be one of the friends that Kevin

was talking about, the kind of person who abandoned someone when things got rough.

"Your eye," I said. "Are you okay?"

He looked up at me. "What? Oh, sure. It's nothing."

There was a smudge of oil on his cheek, just below the black eye. It was indescribably cute. Which made me realize that I didn't want to just hug him. I wanted to *hold* him, and more, like I had before, back when we were boyfriends.

Then I remembered Otto.

I *had* a boyfriend! I had *told* Kevin this. If he had thought that by coming out he was going to change everything, well, he'd been wrong. Nothing was different.

I decided to change the subject. "So how do you jump a car anyway? I can never remember."

Kevin stared at me a second. Then he grinned (impishly, natch). "It's easy. Come here, I'll show you. You have to make sure you do it right, or the battery can explode."

I took a step closer to the engine but still held back. I'd like to say I was worried about the battery exploding, but I was really more afraid of getting too close to Kevin.

"You start with both cars turned off," Kevin said. "Then you connect the positive cable—that's the red one—to the

positive terminal on the dead battery. See, it's marked with a little plus sign?"

I had to shuffle closer to the engine to see what Kevin was talking about. I was standing right next to him now, so close I could actually feel his body heat. I felt like a satellite reentering the earth's atmosphere.

"Okay," Kevin said, "then you connect the other positive end to the positive terminal of the good battery." Since we didn't have a second car, he had to pantomime this part. "Next you take the negative end—the black one—and connect it to the negative side of the bad battery." Kevin did this too. As he worked, I noticed that he had more black grease on his hands. "Finally, you connect the other negative end to the last terminal of the good battery."

This close to him, I could smell Kevin too. It had only been eight months, but I'd already forgotten his complicated mixture of scents: dollar soap, leather from his baseball mitt, and fresh-cut grass.

He turned to face me. "Then you just start the cars."

I turned to face him. Our lips were only inches apart. "Start the cars?" I said, my mouth bone-dry.

"Live car first," he said softly, almost a whisper. "And let it run for a few minutes. Then you can start the dead car."

I wasn't listening. If I ever found myself with a dead

battery, I still wouldn't have any idea what to do. But I did know one thing. Being so close to Kevin was jump-starting my heart. I could feel the sizzle of his electricity right in front of me, could hear it crackling.

No! I thought. I loved *Otto!*

But Otto lived eight hundred miles away. For months he'd been nothing more than flashing blips on a computer screen.

Kevin leaned forward. He was definitely no mere flashing blip. No, he was flesh and blood, and more.

His lips touched mine. The electricity surged between us. But we must have been doing something wrong, because it felt like my head was exploding.

This was totally unacceptable! I had made it very clear to him that he and I couldn't be together! (Except that that had all changed when he came out.)

But Kevin was kissing me. And the embarrassing, totally honest truth is that, yeah, I think maybe I was kissing him back.

CHAPTER SIX

"Russ?" a voice said.

It was Gunnar, standing with Em behind me in the parking lot.

I immediately jerked back from Kevin.

"Kevin needs a jump!" I said loudly.

"Yeah," Em said wryly. "And I can see you were giving him one."

It was a really funny joke, but none of us laughed, not even a little. I think it was because the situation was just so unbelievably not-funny.

Gunnar moved his car closer, so we could get Kevin's running again. Kevin worked in complete silence. I watched it all from one side, unable to move or talk. It was the closest I'd ever come to having an out-of-body experience.

As Kevin backed his car away, he leaned out the window and said to me with a wink, "See you tomorrow."

I didn't answer, but I felt myself sort of wave.

I caught a glimpse of something on the back of my hand. He'd left a grease mark on my skin, and no matter how I rubbed it, it wouldn't come off.

Oh, God, did I feel guilty.

"I can't believe I just did that!" I said to Gunnar and Em, once we were in the car and driving away.

"Calm down," Em said. "Tell us what happened."

I explained everything that had gone on. I told Em the stuff about Kevin's coming out, since she hadn't heard that part before.

"I bet Kevin left his headlights on on purpose," she said. "That dog! He's trying to seduce you."

"Well, it's not going to work!" I said. "He kissed me, I didn't kiss him." This wasn't completely true, since I *had* kissed Kevin back. But Gunnar and Em didn't need to know that.

"I need to tell Otto," I said.

"Maybe," Gunnar said.

"What do you mean?"

"What you need is to figure out what you really want.

And you need to do it fast. It's not fair to lead Otto on. And if you decide you want to break up with him, then you can tell him. But even then, there's no reason to tell him about Kevin. That would just be mean." Gunnar paused for a second, then said, "For the record? I *still* can't believe I'm giving *you* relationship advice. Me! Gunnar! The former loser who couldn't get a girlfriend!"

"Uh, Gunnar?" I said. "Can we stay on topic here?"

"And hel-lo!" Em said. "Girlfriend is sitting in the backseat! Could we also keep a little mystique in this relationship? Don't exactly want to be reminded how you couldn't get a girlfriend."

"Sorry," said Gunnar. To me, he added, "So anyway, you need to pick between Kevin and Otto. And you should try to do it before Otto gets here."

In spite of everything, Gunnar was right on—again. He had a definite future as an advice columnist.

But knowing what you have to do isn't the same thing at all as actually doing it.

That night, I IMed Otto.

> **Smuggler:** Hey you.
>
> **OttoManEmpire:** Hey you. I was just thinking about you!

Smuggler: I was just thinking about you too.

I *had* been thinking about him, but probably not in the way he was thinking about me.

OttoManEmpire: How's it going with your parents?

Smuggler: The same. But now they know about you.

OttoManEmpire: They do?! And they're still okay with letting me come?

Smuggler: Well, they didn't exactly say no. But it didn't go over real well.

This was the understatement of the century.

OttoManEmpire: Geez. How are you doing?

I had to think about this. How *was* I doing, now that things had calmed down a little?

Smuggler: Can I be honest?

OttoManEmpire: Of course!

Smuggler: I feel horrible. Like I'm this terrible person. I know I'm not. Being gay isn't anything to be ashamed of. But they're

my parents. Up till now, they've always been right about everything. This time, they're wrong, but it still FEELS like they're right. Like I've made this huge mistake. Like I have something to be ashamed of. But it's even worse than that, because they're not making me feel bad for anything I've DONE, but for just being who I am. For being the same person I've ALWAYS been. So now I feel twice as bad. First, because it feels like I've made this huge mistake, and second, because I know I've completely disappointed them.

Wow, I thought. Where had all *that* come from? But it was all true. Somehow things were always a lot clearer whenever I talked to Otto.

Smuggler: Does all that make sense?

OttoManEmpire: YES!!! It makes PERFECT sense!! They're your parents! Why would you feel any other way?

That made me smile, to know that Otto had understood.

Smuggler: Do you think they'll ever change? Do you think they'll ever accept me?

OttoManEmpire: I honestly don't know. But it does remind me of a cat we used to have.

Smuggler: A cat?

OttoManEmpire: He used to sit on the mailbox in front of our house. He'd spend the whole day out there, watching the neighborhood. Our whole family used to make fun of him, laughing about why he spent so much time up there, what he could possibly see. Then one day, we heard squealing tires in front of the house. We all went out to see what had happened. There's a greenbelt alongside our house, and a deer must have wandered out from the woods and been hit by a car.

Smuggler: Yuck.

OttoManEmpire: That deer had been killed right in front of our mailbox. The car that hit it hadn't stopped, must have just driven off. So our cat hopped down off the mailbox and climbed up on top of the dead deer. My whole family stood on our

front porch, looking out at the cat standing on top of that huge deer. It looked exactly like the cat had taken down the deer. And so we all just started laughing. That old cat had been right to sit on that mailbox all those months, and our whole family had been dead wrong to make fun of him. Anyway, that cat reminds me of you.

Smuggler: I remind you of a cat on a mailbox? Why?

OttoManEmpire: Because you're exactly where you should be, even if your parents can't see it yet.

Wow! I thought. Otto had *really* understood! I remembered again that moonlight night at camp on the lake in the rowboat. Was this guy a keeper or what?

Smuggler: Otto, I think that's the nicest thing anyone has ever said to me.

OttoManEmpire: Lol!

Smuggler: But there's one gigantic difference between me and that cat.

OttoManEmpire: What's that?

Smuggler: He was all alone on that mailbox. But

I've got you. And I can't imagine being
without you.

I meant every word that I'd typed. I also knew then and
there that I would pick Otto over Kevin any day. So there
was no reason to tell Otto anything at all about Kevin,
because nothing had changed between us, right? He was
the one I wanted.

Otto and I kept typing, sending kissing and hugging
emoticons back and forth and getting gushier by the second.
But I should probably stop the scene here, because if I don't,
you'll quit reading right now in complete disgust.

The next day, the Sunday before Thanksgiving, we had yet
another day of extra work on *Attack of the Soul-Sucking
Brain Zombies*. We were back to one unit, all of us working
with the real director again.

I saw Kevin, but to his credit, he kept his distance. I
think he knew he had crossed some kind of line yesterday
with his under-the-hood seduction. Maybe he was worried
that if he tried to talk to me, I would give him the cold
shoulder. It was a good call, because that was exactly what
I had in mind.

The first shot of the day took place in one of the hallways. They had us half-zombie extras walking back and

forth in front of this vending machine.

Brad, played by Declan McDonnell, heads down the hall, talking to the only other person in the whole school who doesn't seem to be turning into a zombie—a girl named Christy, who wears glasses and slightly baggy clothing and is therefore supposed to be an outcast like Brad, but who is really played by this stunningly beautiful twenty-four-year-old actress. Brad and Christy stare at the half-zombies listing and groaning all around them, wondering if they're seeing things or what.

Still absorbed by the appearance of the other students, Brad and Christy stop at the vending machine. Brad puts some money in. But when he finally looks up to pick something from the machine, he sees that all the candy and chips have been replaced by bloody body parts—disembodied hands and feet and arms and organs. As he and Christy are gaping at the machine in horror, the captain of the football team, a half-zombie, walks up to it and slams the buttons with one hand, causing a messy human forearm to fall into the dispenser. Then he walks away gnawing on the bone.

I still hadn't seen a script or anything, but I was finally starting to piece together the plot of *Attack of the Soul-Sucking Brain Zombies*. Declan McDonnell's character has arrived at this new high school, only to find all the kids strictly divided into impenetrable cliques, with everyone

sort of lumbering through their days. Get it? Basically, they're already mindless zombies?

But as the days go by, the students start turning into *actual* zombies—with yellow skin and mussed-up hair. So Brad teams up with Christy to try to figure out who's turning the whole school into zombies, and why. That's what the scene at the vending machine was all about: they're finally realizing that, no, it's not all in their imaginations.

They kept shooting the vending machine scene over and over. I was still ignoring Kevin, but around the fifth take, I couldn't help but notice that he suddenly seemed to be getting awfully cozy with one of the other zombie-jocks.

Or maybe they were just talking. I mean, since Min, Gunnar, and I were ignoring him, Kevin had to talk to someone, right? I couldn't tell if the other guy was good-looking or not, because of the yellow makeup and messed-up hair. I hadn't paid any attention to him before, but now I couldn't help but notice that he did have a pretty good body.

I tried to put them both out of my mind. Before the next shot, I talked with Min, Gunnar, and Em.

"I have a question," I said.

"Yes?" Min said.

"Has anyone figured out what a brain zombie is yet?"

Min smiled. "Not a clue. It hasn't been mentioned in any of the scenes I've been in."

"I *still* say it's explained somewhere in the script," Gunnar mumbled.

Suddenly Kevin laughed. I turned. He was standing across the hall with that other zombie-jock. The guy had his hand up against the wall, leaning into it, exactly the way a guy leans into the wall when he's hitting on a girl. But Kevin didn't seem to mind. He was laughing and talking, so engrossed that he didn't even notice me staring at him.

Well, what difference did it make if he *was* being hit on by another guy? I wasn't interested in Kevin anyway, right? I didn't even want to talk to him. But it did sort of speak to Kevin's state of mind. I mean, if he was so desperate to get back together with me—so desperate that he'd become a movie extra just to get close to me—what was he doing letting himself be hit on by another guy? He had to know that I'd notice. Was he trying to make me jealous? Or was he just so weak-willed that when some random guy hit on him, he was powerless to resist?

I decided to block Kevin and his new "friend" out of my mind completely. Instead, I concentrated on Declan McDonnell. Him, I did want to talk to again, desperately. I didn't really expect to, but I decided why not swing by that bathroom where I'd seen him before? So I did.

Six times.

Every time we had a break or even an obviously long pause between shots, I went to that bathroom. And every time, I found myself alone. It was stupid, I know. Of course I was never going to talk to Declan McDonnell again. I'd been lucky to talk to him once!

When I went back to that bathroom a seventh time, he was there. He was standing at one of the thirty urinals, just zipping up.

"Oh!" I said.

"Oh," he said. "Hello again."

He picked up a silver dagger that I hadn't noticed sitting on top of the urinal. It had jewels in the handle and every-

thing.

"What's that?" I asked.

"Just a prop. What I use to kill the zombies in the last part of the movie. I find it in a drawer in the principal's desk."

Taking the dagger with him, he crossed to the sinks to wash his hands.

"Hey, can I ask you a question?" I said. I didn't really have a question in mind, but I figured I had to say something, or he'd fly away again.

"Huh?" he said. "Sure, I guess." He finished washing and started drying his hands.

"What's the secret of high school?"

I have no idea what made me say this. It was just the first thing that popped into my head. I guess it was because Declan McDonnell was always playing high school students. He had to know the secret, right?

He shrugged. "Beats me. I didn't even go to high school."

"What?"

"It's true. I dropped out my sophomore year, when I started getting jobs on television. I had on-set tutors. I always wondered if I missed out."

"You didn't," I said quickly. "Seriously. Not at *all*. Trust me on this."

He laughed. "Well, it is ironic. I've spent the last ten years playing high school students."

"You're twenty-six?" I said, surprised. I knew he probably wasn't a teenager, but I had no idea he was that old.

"Maybe even more like twenty-eight." He winked. "Don't tell anyone, okay?" He looked at me. "So you hate high school, huh?"

"Well, *hate* is a strong word. So I'd say, yeah, it's perfect to describe how I feel about high school."

He snorted. "You're pretty smart," he said. "Anyone ever tell you that?"

"Yeah. It's part of the reason why I've always been known as Mr. Popularity at my school."

He laughed one more time, and I wondered why I

couldn't ever be this charming around guys who weren't untouchable angels.

"I didn't go to high school, but I read a lot of high school scripts, so I've learned a few things," Declan McDonnell said. "You really want the secret?"

"Yeah," I said. "Totally."

He fingered the pommel of the dagger in his hand. Fake rubies and emeralds glinted in the fluorescent light. "Adults think they know what's going on," he said, "but they actually have no idea."

I thought about this. "I know that's a movie cliché, but that's actually true."

"The less you care about popularity, the cooler you are," he continued.

"I can't deny it," I said.

"Finally, high school is about the future."

"What?"

"Think about it," he said. "Every year in high school is a new one, a chance to reinvent yourself, a chance to try something different. And every year leads you closer to that ultimate adventure, graduation. When you've played as many valedictorians as I have, and given all those graduation speeches, you know that high school is about looking ahead. Believe me."

I thought about this last one. It actually made a lot of sense.

"Well," Declan McDonnell said at last. "I should be getting back."

"Right," I said. "And thanks! A lot."

"Sure."

This time I watched him leave, disappearing up that little flight of steps. It didn't make him any more human, though. Declan McDonnell was the kind of angel who didn't need wings to fly.

When I got home that night, I felt better than I had in a long time. It was partly my second encounter with Declan McDonnell. But it was also the fact that in three days Otto was going to be here, and then everything would be clear. I was certain I'd see him, and it would feel just like old times. Everything would be right again, and I'd know that we could make this long-distance-relationship thing work. Or maybe, just maybe, it wouldn't feel right. Either way, things would finally be settled.

For the time being, I'd forgotten all about my parents. Let's face it: they were being total babies about this whole gay thing, and I had more important things to worry about.

Unfortunately, my parents were waiting for me again,

right inside the front door. What had they been doing, standing in the foyer?

"What," I said. I could tell just by looking that whatever they wanted to say, it wasn't good. For one thing, there was more dirt under my mom's fingernails.

"He can't come," my mom said.

"What?" I said.

"That boy. The one from summer camp."

"Otto?" She knew his name. We'd been talking about Otto's visit for weeks. But now that she knew I was gay and he was my boyfriend, he had suddenly become "that boy."

"Mom," I said. "What are you talking about?"

"Your mother and I talked about it," my dad said. "He can't come here for Thanksgiving break."

"But he's already bought his ticket!" I protested. "It's all planned! It's *been* planned!"

"Look," my mom said, "did you really think that we were going to let you bring your boyfriend into this house to stay with you?"

"But—!"

"There is no 'but'!" my mom said. "He can't stay here, and that's final!"

CHAPTER SEVEN

I DON'T KNOW WHY I was so surprised. It should have been obvious when my mom had learned Otto was my boyfriend that she wasn't going to let him come and stay with us. I guess I'd deliberately avoided doing the math.

But *now* what did I do? I honestly didn't know. I *needed* Otto to come for Thanksgiving, not just because I really, really wanted to see him, but also because I had to figure out where this relationship of ours was heading. Now my parents were saying he couldn't come. Living so far apart, we weren't going to be seeing much of each other anyway, but now the one chance we had was gone.

"Why doesn't he stay here with me?" Gunnar said. Gunnar lived right near me, and I'd gone over there to bitch about what my parents had done.

"What?" I said, perking up.

Gunnar shrugged. "Well, why not? He's my friend too." This was true. We'd both met Otto at the same time, at camp that summer. "I'll have to ask my parents," Gunnar went on, "but I'm sure it'll be okay. I'll tell them Otto got a free ticket at the last minute or something. Or I might even tell 'em the truth!"

"Are you serious about this?"

"Why not? We can pick him up at the airport together, and we can even eat Thanksgiving here. But then you guys can get together too. You can even spend the night over here, downstairs."

"But my parents—"

"What about them?"

I thought about this. Technically, my parents hadn't said Otto couldn't come visit—just that he couldn't stay with *them*. And they were being completely unreasonable and homophobic, so why should I care what they said anyway?

I let myself smile. "Gunnar, you're a genius! Let's do it!"

Two days later, Gunnar, Em, Min, and I picked up Otto at the airport. We had to wait for him outside the security gate. So close to Thanksgiving, it was a madhouse. I was jumpy, excited to see him, but also anxious that somehow things had changed between us.

I stared into the crowd of people rushing at us through the security gate. After a while, everyone started to look the same. It's not that the individuals stopped looking different—old, young, fat, skinny, black, white, whatever. It's just that after about a minute or so, all I saw were about fifteen "types" of people, like one of those old cartoons where the character is running, and you can tell they're recycling the background.

Finally, the crowd parted, and Otto emerged. He looked a little dazed, dragging his suitcase but trying to figure out where to go next. Then he saw us, and his face lit up like a halogen lamp. He looked like I remembered, but more so, if that makes any sense. And he looked nothing whatsoever like anyone else around him.

No, really. For one thing, he was really cute. His smile reached out and really grabbed you. And if he didn't snag you with his smile, he got you with his eyes, which are this amazing brownish burgundy. He also had this nice trim bod, if I do say so myself.

For another thing, he had this huge scar that covered one half of his face (and others on his shoulder and back, except they were obviously hidden by his clothes). The scar on his face looked sort of like a swirl with his eye in the middle. When he was seven years old, he'd had an accident with some gasoline. But this didn't make him any less

handsome. In my mind, it made him look better, because it was something unique, part of him and him alone.

He let go of his bag, stepped forward, and kissed me. I was surprised for a second, but then I kissed him right back. He smelled like juniper bushes (and tasted like ginger ale).

I knew people were staring at us, two teenage boys kissing. But I guess Otto with his scar was used to being stared at, because he didn't seem to notice.

I didn't mind either. On the contrary, I was busting with pride.

Once we got to Gunnar's, Otto and I went for a walk so we could be alone and talk. It was after ten on a November night, but if the air was cold, I sure didn't feel it. The best part was just being able to hold his hand—though we did have to let go of each other and step apart every time a car drove by. (It's one thing to be stared at in airports; it's something else entirely to have beer bottles thrown in your direction from passing pickup trucks. But that's young gay love for you.)

"God, I've missed you so much!" Otto said.

"Me too," I said.

"How much?"

I looked over at him. "What?"

"How much have you missed me?" He smirked mis-

chievously, so I figured he wanted me to say something romantic.

I glanced up at the sky, and then I had it. "I've missed you like the earth misses the moon!" A second later, I added, more quietly, "You know that the moon used to be part of the earth, right? They learned that from moon rocks they collected back in the seventies."

Otto didn't say anything, just smiled. So I added, "Wow, romantic sayings lose a lot when you have to explain the science behind them, don't they?"

Otto laughed, so I laughed too.

"Okay," I said. "How about this? I've missed you like the beach misses the wave."

"How does the beach miss the wave?" Otto asked. "It only has to wait a minute or so for the next wave."

"Well, not at low tide. Because there's a twelve-hour period when—"

"More science, huh?"

"Everyone's a critic! Well, this is harder than it seems. You try."

"Okay." He thought for a second. "I've missed you like a desert misses the rain. There. Nice and simple, and you don't need to know the scientific explanation."

"Yeah," I said, "but it's a total cliché."

"Oh, yeah? Like a beach missing the wave isn't a

cliché? Okay, you don't want clichés? Well, then, I've missed you like a decapitated head misses its neck!"

"Definitely not a cliché," I agreed. "But not very romantic either!"

Otto snickered. "Take your pick! You can't have everything."

"Well, in that case," I said, "I've missed you like a frog misses the ozone layer!"

"And I've missed you like a loose eyeball misses its socket!"

"Ewww!" I said, laughing. "Well, I've missed you like the surface of Mars misses an atmosphere!"

"And I've missed you like a disemboweled body misses its, well, bowels!"

We were both laughing so hard now we could barely talk. I felt so good, like I was completely weightless, and Otto and I were bobbing around giddily up among the clouds. All the stuff with my parents, and Kevin, it just no longer existed.

I suddenly thought about what Declan McDonnell had said about high school being about the future. That's what it felt like right then. But barreling into the future all the time, not to mention bobbing around weightless, is very disorienting.

I lost my balance for a second and bumped up against Otto.

The moment I touched him, I had the strangest sensation. You know how they say that people sometimes live in their head? At that moment, it was like I was living in my skin. That was the only part of me that existed. My skin had never felt so sensitive before, every inch of it, tingling and aware. It was different from the electricity that had passed between Kevin and me when he'd been working on his dead battery. That had definitely gotten my attention, but this felt deeper somehow, not merely physical.

Otto was clearly experiencing all this too. "Wow!" he said, eyes wide. "What was *that*?"

"I don't know," I said.

I lifted the palm of my hand, and Otto pressed his against mine. I wasn't just feeling my actual skin anymore. Before that moment, I hadn't believed in auras or spirits or even souls in the literal sense, but I believed in them now. I could actually *feel* mine, like a second skin, and maybe even more alive. I could feel Otto's too, pressing up against me, warm and soothing.

I leaned forward to kiss him. When his tongue slipped inside my mouth, I gasped. His soul was suddenly inside mine too, something I had never felt before.

I wanted to stay that way forever, but Otto broke the kiss far too soon.

"Wait," he said. "What's that smell?"

"Huh?" I said, disoriented again, missing his soul and his tongue.

"It smells like a swamp. Methane or something."

I looked around and suddenly realized where we were. We'd walked to the park with the stinky picnic gazebo, the place where I'd met Kevin the first time, and the week earlier as well. Why had I brought Otto here? I hadn't intended to. We'd just been walking aimlessly. But my skin wasn't aware and tingly anymore. And remember when I said I felt all weightless and giddy? I felt the pull of gravity again. I suddenly wanted more than anything to get away from this place.

"What is it?" Otto said, sensing the change in me.

"Nothing," I said, stepping away. "Let's just keep walking, okay?"

The next day, Thursday, I had Thanksgiving with my parents (and some relatives) early in the afternoon, but I barely ate. I also pretended to be all miffed and sullen (which wasn't hard). So when I said "I'm going over to Gunnar's," my parents were perfectly happy to see me go.

When I got to Gunnar's house, he and his family and Otto were just starting dinner. Min and Em had also stopped by. Gunnar's mom put us all at this table by ourselves in the

kitchen, along with Gunnar's bespectacled, eleven-year-old cousin Myron. For the first time in my life, I didn't mind being at the "kiddies' table." Even with Myron there, it was like my friends and I were having our own Thanksgiving meal, complete with all the fixings. We even had our own little turkey, but I was sitting facing the hollowed-out end where the stuffing had been, so it felt a little like I was being mooned.

"Gunnar," I said, dishing up the cranberry corn bread stuffing, "this is great! Thanks for having us."

"Thank my mom," he said. "All I did was make the papier-mâché cornucopia out on the grown-ups' table. And that was back in the sixth grade!"

We all laughed and started chowing down. The turkey was moist, the broccoli crunched, and the gravy had a creamy rosemary flavor.

But as we ate, we talked—about everything under the sun.

For example, I told everyone an idea I'd had a few months before, when I was weeding in our yard.

"There should be something called National Dandelion Day," I said. "On one day, every person in the world goes out and digs up all the dandelions in his yard at the very same time. Then there'd be no dandelions to go to seed and

send their little evil parachutes out into the world. It would solve the dandelion problem forever. No one would ever have to weed again! Assuming everyone got the roots. You have to get all the root, or the damn thing grows back."

"It wouldn't work," Min said.

"Why not?" Gunnar asked. "I'd be into it."

"Yeah," said Myron, Gunnar's eleven-year-old cousin. "Why not?"

"Well," Min said, "there'd be plenty of jackasses who wouldn't do it. You know, all the idiots who rant and rave about how they don't want anyone telling them what to do with 'their' land? So they wouldn't weed their yards. And they'd sit on their porches with their shotguns to make sure no one else weeded their yards either. So their dandelions would keep growing, and then they'd go to seed, and they'd screw the whole thing up."

"Min's right," Em said. "Some people have no idea about the common good. They bitch about low-flow toilets and they go out and buy a huge, expensive SUV and then flip out about the three-cent gas tax that's needed to pay for all the pollution and congestion they're causing. It's like they think they're the only people in the world."

"I used the bathroom on the plane over here," Otto said. "I went in right after this hotshot businessman-type.

But when I got in there, I saw he'd peed all over the toilet seat. It was completely disgusting. He couldn't even have bothered lifting the seat. It never occurred to him that women were going to use that thing, and old and disabled people who might not be able to bend down and clean it first. Or maybe he just didn't care."

"They need a new sign in airplane bathrooms," Gunnar said. "Rather than the one that says 'As a courtesy to the next passenger, please wipe down the basin after each use.' It should say 'As a courtesy to the next passenger, please don't piss all over the damn bathroom!'"

It was funny, and everyone laughed except me. I wasn't sure why I didn't.

We kept eating, and eventually we moved on to talking about which was the world's best amusement park ride.

"Oh, Tower of Terror!" Gunnar said. "At Disney World. No contest. There are higher drop rides, but none of them have Tower of Terror's atmosphere."

"I like the Haunted Mansion," Em said.

"Oh, yes," said Min. "That's a classic."

"It doesn't have as many of those cheesy animatronic robots, like Pirates of the Caribbean," Em said. "So it seems less dated. Plus it has a better sense of humor."

"But you've got to love those fireflies on Pirates of the

Caribbean," Min said.

"Indiana Jones is good," said Otto, playing footsie with me under the table. "I used to like those simulator rides, like Body War or Star Tours. But they just don't hold up. You ride 'em once, and then it just feels like you're being jerked around in the back of a truck."

"There's this ride called Poseidon's Fury?" said Gunnar's cousin Myron. "At Islands of Adventure in Orlando. You go into this temple, then down into the city of Atlantis. And at the end, they turn this huge room into a tiny room really, really fast! It is so cool!"

"Tower of Terror!" Gunnar repeated. "It's *clearly* the best! I can't believe you guys can't see that."

Weirdly, this talk of amusement park rides was depressing me. I wasn't sure why, because ordinarily I loved amusement park rides. I reached for the relish tray, but the baby corn was all gone, and that made me sad too.

Next we talked about gay teen movies.

"They all suck," Otto said.

"Except for *Beautiful Thing*," Em added.

And that was pretty much all we had to say on *that* topic!

Finally, we even had sort of a Thanksgiving-esque conversation about everything that had happened to all of us lately, and what we were grateful for.

"It's been an amazing year," Min said reflectively.

"Think about it all. This time last year, we hadn't even started the Geography Club."

"And I hadn't met Em," Gunnar said, smiling at her.

"And I hadn't met Russel," said Otto.

"You'll meet someone too," I said to Min, worried she might feel left out not having someone in her life.

"Uh-huh," she said, taking a big drink of her ice water.

Suddenly Gunnar said, "I don't want this to end."

Em looked around the tabletop. "Too late," she said drolly. She was right. Like six Very Hungry Caterpillars, we'd chomped our way through every little morsel of food. The turkey, of course, had been picked completely clean.

"I don't mean dinner," Gunnar said. "I mean this." He nodded around the table. "Us. I really like things the way they are right now. I don't want to just graduate from college, get a job, and buy a house in the suburbs." He glanced out toward the dining room. The conversation of the adults sounded like an otherworldly moan. Gunnar softened his voice. "I look at my parents' lives, at how boring they are. They don't have friends—they have dinner party guests! I don't want to ever be like them. Do you think we have to?"

"No!" said Myron. We all looked at him. "We can have whatever lives we want. If people have boring lives, it's because they *choose* to have boring lives. If their friends are

stupid, it's because they *choose* stupid friends. We don't have to end up like our parents. We *don't*."

Myron was only eleven years old, but he was surprisingly precocious. No one could have said it better.

And it was right then that I realized why I was suddenly feeling so sad. It wasn't the conversation we'd been having, not even this latest, serious part about growing up and turning boring. It was because right then, at that table at least, my life was perfect. I had told Declan McDonnell the truth about high school—that I hated it. But that was just the school part. The rest of my life was pretty amazing. And right then, I was with a guy I loved and who loved me, and friends I loved and who loved me too. Like that night on the lake in the rowboat with Otto, life at that moment was absolutely perfect.

But it wasn't going to stay perfect for long. For one thing, I'd have to go home to parents who I now knew didn't love me the way I was, or accept me unconditionally. And as for the guy I loved, he was about to become MIA. On Saturday, forty-four hours from right then, Otto had to go home. Who knew when I'd see him again? And that was just about the saddest thing imaginable.

Yes, yes, it was unbelievably stupid to be sad about something that hadn't even happened yet, to be ruining the brief time we did have together. But I couldn't help it. I felt

I was going to cry. I couldn't imagine going back to
I'd been before I'd come out, before we'd created the
ography Club. It's one thing to be sad that you don't
ve the one thing you desperately want. It might be even
worse to get what you want for a little while, only to have it
taken away from you.

"Let's make a vow," Em said. "Let's promise each other
right here and now that we won't ever turn boring. And if
we do, we give the others permission to come make us do
something completely crazy!"

We all laughed, even me, because now it would have
been obvious if I hadn't. And then we all agreed to Em's
pledge.

Afterward, we talked and laughed some more, and Otto
kept playing footsie with me under the table. I tried to pretend I was having the same good time that everyone else was
having. But inside, I felt like that turkey carcass in the middle
of the table—with a big hole right in the middle of my chest.

CHAPTER EIGHT

THE NEXT DAY, FRIDAY of Thanksgiving vacation, we all
went back to work as extras on *Attack of the Soul-Sucking*
110 *Brain Zombies*. Otto joined us, bringing the permission
form signed by his parents.

"Can I ask a question?" Otto asked Gunnar, Em, and
me that morning on the way to the school.

"Sure," I said.

"What's a brain zombie?"

Em and I burst into laughter.

"No one knows!" I said.

"We still haven't figured that out," Em said. "It hasn't
come up in any of the scenes we've been in."

This time, Gunnar didn't say a word, just sulked a little.

That morning we all became full-fledged zombies for
the very first time, with costuming and makeup and

everything. There were about twenty-five zombie extras that day, but only six makeup artists, so they were definitely working overtime.

I was one of the last people out of makeup. Wardrobe had dressed me in a T-shirt and white long-sleeved shirt, all shredded and bloody, and geeky, computer-nerd pants covered with some kind of fake dirt that smelled like chalk dust. Then they'd plastered my face with a base of green makeup (more olive, really) and used something called spirit gum to paste these fake scabs and boils all over my cheeks and forehead. And they'd oiled my hair and messed it up again, and given me this set of rotting, yellow teeth, which I could slip in and out of my mouth, but which made it so I could still talk. Finally, they'd glued half of this plastic calculator to me, so it looked like someone had jammed it into the side of my head.

In short, I looked like a walking, slowly rotting corpse. True, they'd pegged me for a computer nerd (again), but I guess I couldn't have everything.

The first shot took place right outside the front doors of the school. The school bell was supposed to ring, and then all we zombie-students were to come staggering out. The doors had been rigged to burst off their hinges so it looked like we were doing it.

Kevin was there, waiting with the other extras. He'd been made up as a full zombie now too. They'd put him in a torn, moldy-looking letterman's jacket, and he carried a blood-spattered baseball bat (which was appropriate, given that he did play baseball). His makeup was like mine, except they'd also made it look like he'd had his neck ripped open and blood had dripped down onto his shirt.

"You look great," I said, before I could stop myself. "How'd they do that to your neck?"

He stared at me with a completely straight face. "Whaddaya mean? Do what? Hey, what's taking them so long with the makeup anyway? Aren't you getting tired of waiting?"

I smiled.

"Hey, I see you got some new clothes," he went on. "A big improvement over what you usually wear."

"Thanks," I said. "Thanks a lot." It was still weird to see Kevin in full zombie makeup, but what was interesting was how quickly I got used to it.

He narrowed his eyes. "Something else looks different about you. You get a new haircut? And your teeth. You get them whitened or something?"

I laughed. Kevin could be funny. I glanced around for the guy who had been hitting on him that Sunday, but I didn't see him anywhere.

Kevin tilted his head to one side and made to scratch his torn-up throat. "Man, my neck is itching. I think I have a rash or something. You see anything?"

At that, I admit I cracked up. It felt so good just to laugh. I still hadn't shaken that horrible emptiness I'd felt at Thanksgiving dinner the night before, and I guess I was desperate to forget all that.

Then I happened to look to one side. Otto was done with his makeup now too, and he'd joined us on the set.

He was looking right at Kevin and me.

They'd made Otto a zombie-jock too, like Kevin, except he was wearing a cracked and bloody football helmet and carrying a deflated pigskin. They'd turned his real scar into a fake injury, so it looked like half his face was falling off.

"Wow, you look great," I said when Otto joined Kevin and me.

"Yeah!" Kevin said. "That scar looks really real!"

"It *is* real," I said. "Otto's a burn survivor."

"Really?" Kevin said, not missing a beat. "Hey, that's great!" I wasn't sure if Kevin was talking about the fact that Otto had survived the burn, or that he'd been willing to come and be an extra in a horror film. But either way, I was impressed that he hadn't gotten all flustered.

"Thanks," Otto said.

"Kevin?" I said. "This is my boyfriend, Otto."

"Oh," Kevin said, but he didn't say anything else. Now he *was* flustered. That was ironic.

This is stupid, I thought. I should just say something. But I couldn't think of anything to say. I guess I was flustered too. Otto didn't say anything either. It was a three-way fluster.

We just stood there with no one saying anything. How long was this awkward silence going to continue? It occurred to me that I could tell Otto that Kevin had once been my boyfriend too, but if anything could have made that moment even more awkward, that was probably it.

It was the movie director who finally broke the interminable silence. "Okay!" he called. "Let's have a rehearsal!"

Thank God! I thought. It was like Aslan from *The Chronicles of Narnia* had breathed on us, turning us from stone into real people again.

"Okay," the director said. "You're full zombies now, right? Let's see you act like them. Stiff legs, arms outstretched, the works! We'll be rerecording the zombies in the studio, but growl anyway—it'll help you get into character."

We all moved into position.

"Rolling!" the director said, even though we knew it was just a rehearsal. "And *action!*"

The fake school bell sounded. Together, we zombies shambled forward, groaning and lurching. At the first touch of the lead zombies, the front doors exploded off their hinges, flying off to the sides.

As we were crowding out onto the steps, one of the zombie-jocks slammed against me with his shoulder, groaning gleefully.

"And . . . *cut!*" said the director.

Otto immediately turned to the "jock" who had knocked against me.

"What was *that* about?" Otto asked.

"Huh?" the jock said.

"You almost flattened my friend!"

"We're supposed to," the guy said defensively. "The director told the jocks to pick on the nerds."

"When?" Otto asked. "I didn't hear him say that."

"Before," he said. "In one of the other scenes."

Otto thought for a second. "Well," he said firmly, "if the director wants us to do that kind of thing now, he'll tell us."

I couldn't help but be reminded of how Kevin hadn't spoken up before, when this same guy had started picking on us "nerds." Sure, he'd hesitated, but then he'd joined right in. Otto, meanwhile, was completely immune to this kind of peer pressure.

Soon the cameras were rolling again, but this time none of the zombie-jocks bumped me at all.

Later, during a break, Otto asked me, "So who's that guy?"

"Who?" I said, even though I knew exactly who he meant.

"That guy we were talking to before."

"His name is Kevin. Didn't I introduce you?"

"Yeah, you did. But who is he? How do you know him?"

"He's just a friend." I thought for a second. "Well, actually, he used to be my boyfriend."

"That's *the* Kevin?" At camp, I'd told Otto all about him.

"Uh, yeah."

"I thought you weren't talking to him anymore. That he didn't want to come out, so that made it impossible." Apparently, I'd told Otto *all* about him. I'd forgotten that.

"Oh," I said. "Yeah. Well, we *weren't* talking, not until he signed up to be an extra in the movie too. Then we started talking again."

"Doesn't he worry about being seen with you?"

What was with the third degree from Otto? But of course I knew.

"Um, Kevin came out," I admitted.

"When was this?"

"Just last week, actually."

Otto didn't say anything for a second. I could tell he was surprised.

"Why didn't you tell me any of this?" he said at last.

Why *hadn't* I told him any of this? At first it was because I wasn't sure if I still had feelings for Kevin, and I hadn't wanted to hurt Otto's feelings. But why hadn't it occurred to me that Otto was going to be a zombie extra too, so he'd eventually figure things out? I should have filled him in. Now I'd made him all suspicious.

"It just never came up," I said. "It's not any big deal."

This wasn't the whole truth. Then again, the issue here really wasn't Kevin. It was Otto, and the fact that he lived so far away.

Otto stared at me. "Russel," he said, "what's going on? I'm really trying not to be all clingy and insecure. But there's obviously something going on between you and Kevin that you're not telling me about."

"There's nothing going on!" I said. "It was all a misunderstanding!" Why was it that telling one sort-of lie always meant you had to tell a whole bunch more?

Otto sighed. "Okay, whatever. But that doesn't explain why you've been acting all distant."

I froze. How do you respond to the accusation that you're

being distant without either (a) seeming more distant, or (b) confirming that you *are* being distant? But finally I nodded. If there was any time for the truth, this was it.

"I'm just really sad that you have to leave," I said to Otto. "I can't get it out of my mind. You just got here! And I know it'll be months until I get to see you again. That is, if I *ever* get to see you again, which is going to be tough the way my parents are talking."

"Well, there's always next summer. I'll come back for camp."

"Next summer! That's *forever*."

"What are you saying?" Otto said. "You want to break up?"

"No!" I said. But I'd said it too loudly, like I was trying to convince myself along with Otto. "No," I said again.

"Then what *do* you want?"

And that was the thing. I still didn't know. Which was totally unfair to Otto. How could I be honest with him when I still hadn't been honest with myself?

For the time being, I decided to change the subject.

"I want *you*, of course," I said. "It's this thing with my parents. It has me all mixed up."

Otto nodded sympathetically. "It's okay. I understand." But for the first time, I wondered if maybe he wasn't telling me the whole truth either.

* * *

That afternoon, production assistants shepherded us into the cafeteria for another shot. They divided us into groups of about five each according to our costumes and directed all of us to different lunch tables. A fake corpse lay limply on the top of each table.

I spotted Min on the other side of the room. They'd dressed her as a cheerleader again—a *zombie*-cheerleader, with green skin and blood-spattered pom-poms. I waved, but she was staring over at the band-geek table, so she didn't notice me.

The director spoke to us all, explaining how we were supposed to pretend to be chomping down on the fake corpse in front of us. Then Brad and Christy, the two main characters, would come in and see us and say some dialogue. The scene was obviously a joke. It was supposed to be just like lunch at a normal high school, with all the jocks at one table, the cheerleaders at another table, the band geeks at another table, and the computer nerds at yet another table. Only the jocks and cheerleaders and band geeks and computer nerds are all zombies, and rather than eating lunches, we're eating human corpses. Get it?

"And make it real!" the director said. "Get right down into those corpses with your hands and faces!"

We did a rehearsal, then stood around waiting for

Declan McDonnell and the actress playing Christy, and for the lighting designer to finish positioning the lights.

The only person I knew in my little cluster of computer-nerd zombies was Gunnar, which was just as well. I'd wanted to talk to him anyway.

"Here's a fun fact," Gunnar said, looking down at the corpse on our table. "The same company that makes many of Hollywood's fake corpses also makes a line of life-size sex dolls."

I interrupted him. "Gunnar, I think I screwed up."

"Now what?" The makeup artist had made it look like someone had jammed a set of Dungeons and Dragons dice into his forehead.

I told Gunnar about the conversation I'd had with Otto.

"Oops," he said. "That's not good."

I appreciated his not saying "I told you so" about needing to figure out what I wanted before I said anything to Otto.

"So what do I do?" I asked. "What should I tell him?"

But before he could say anything, the director called to us from over by the cameras. "Rolling!" he called. "And . . . action!" Brad and Christy had arrived.

Gunnar and I and the other computer-nerd zombies bent down and started pretending like we were eating the fake corpse. Ours was a middle-aged fat guy in gym shorts

and a T-shirt—the gym instructor (a nice touch, I thought, since we were all computer nerds). The body smelled like latex and Vaseline, but it was eerily realistic-looking: wet and glistening. We could even dig in to actual plastic entrails.

For a second, I felt kind of stupid, smelling that latex and making growling noises that I knew no one would ever really hear.

But then a funny thing happened. I sort of got into the moment. We all looked pretty real, and the body did too. So suddenly I *was* a zombie. There was nothing I wanted more than to rip chunks of flesh off the luscious, bloody pile of fat in front of me. I even lifted a bloody arm and started gnawing on it, growling all the while.

It's not like I have this secret hankering for human flesh. Mostly I think it was just fun to not be me for a second.

A minute or so later, the director said, "And . . . *cut!* Excellent! Good work, zombies!"

And in a flash, I was my old, non-zombie self again. For better or for worse.

I looked over at Gunnar. "Well?" I asked him, meaning the question I'd asked him before, about what I should say to Otto.

He thought for a second. Then he said, "Tastes like chicken."

"Huh?"

He nodded down at the corpse. "The body?"

Finally, I clued in. "Gunnar!" I whacked him on the shoulder. But I laughed too.

"So," he said at last. "You're asking me for relationship advice yet again, huh?"

"Yes," I said, "and I'd appreciate it if this time you skipped the little happy dance and we went right to the advice. You're two for two right now, you know. Don't blow it."

"Well, you're in luck. Because I figured you'd come to me for advice again, so I prepared. How about, 'Love is a great risk, but not loving is the even greater risk'? Or, 'To live without love is not really to live at all.'"

"What'd you do?" I said. "Break open a bunch of fortune cookies?"

"Yeah, actually. But I also thought of a story to tell you."

I sighed. "Okay, let's hear it." But to tell the truth, Gunnar was making me smile, as usual.

"You know how my family always goes to Echo Lake for vacation?"

I nodded. This was a little lake with cabins about a hundred miles from where we lived.

"Well," he went on, "a couple of years ago, I was up there, and I decided to go for a walk in the woods by

myself. Stupid, I know, but I was fourteen, so what can you do? Anyway, the trail was really faint, but I kept walking all afternoon. Finally, I decided to turn around, but almost immediately I came to this fork in the trail. I didn't remember any fork in the trail, so I started to panic. Which was the way home? I didn't know. The two paths looked exactly the same."

"So what did you do?" I said.

"Well, I knew that buried somewhere in my head was the right answer. And if it wasn't, maybe there was some force outside myself—God or the spirit of the forest or whatever—who could give me the answer. So I cleared my head and stared at the two trails. I stood there for the longest time. And finally I knew. I went down the trail on the right."

"And you'd picked the right one."

"Nah," Gunnar said, "I picked wrong. I ended up in this nettles patch, and that was the time I got those ticks, and then later I got sick, and I was sure I had Lyme disease."

"Gunnar!" I cried. "What kind of story is that! You picked the wrong trail?"

"Did I?" Gunnar said. "I'm standing here, aren't I?"

I stared at him. "What do you mean?"

"I mean, obviously I made it back to the cabins. I lived, right?"

"Yeah, but you walked through nettles and ticks, and you thought you had Lyme disease! If you'd gone the other way, none of that would have happened."

"Oh, yeah, the other path would have been a much better choice. But at least I picked one. Because if I hadn't, I'd still be standing up in those woods."

Finally, I saw what he was getting at. Sometimes there's a choice you don't think about—the choice of whether or not to decide. At this point, one way or another, I finally had to decide between Otto and Kevin.

I had to admit it once and for all: Gunnar gave damn good advice.

124

Kevin or Otto. Why couldn't I decide? Well, because it was a *hard* decision, that's why! Give me a break.

But I *had* to decide. Gunnar was right about that.

I loved Otto. He was right for me. That was obvious whenever I spent time with him. And he was such a thoroughly decent guy, the kind of guy who always did the right thing, which was no small matter when it came to boyfriends. But the big "but" was that he lived eight hundred miles away. When you thought about it, that made him not much of a boyfriend at all. He was more like a character in a book—someone you "love," but can't cuddle up to.

Meanwhile, Kevin *was* real. Maybe the only reason I wasn't choosing him was because I didn't want to feel guilty about Otto. But guilt was no reason to stay together with a guy. On the other hand, Kevin was flawed. He was charming and handsome, which are not the worst boyfriend-qualities in the world, but he wasn't strong. I'd trusted him once before, and he'd really jerked me around. Sure, he'd come out to the whole school, but when push came to shove, he usually didn't do the right thing.

I knew what I needed to do. I had to talk with Declan McDonnell. Yes, I wanted just to bask in his presence again. But I also wanted to ask him what to do. He'd already proven to be pretty wise, my own bathroom angel. He alone would have the answer I sought. (And maybe he could also tell me what the hell a "brain zombie" was!)

I went back to the restroom where we'd met those two times before. This time I was certain that he would be there.

He wasn't. I was all alone.

"Great," I said out loud. "Just great." It echoed off the cold tile. Well, at least I could try again later in the day.

I turned to go, but as I did, I caught a glimpse of something along the wall.

A zombie watched me gloomily.

It wasn't Declan McDonnell or one of the other zombie

extras. It was me, in full zombie makeup, reflected in one of the bathroom's cracked and cloudy mirrors.

And that's when I knew the answer. Otto or Kevin? It was so obvious!

I had to tell the guy I had chosen. But I couldn't do it at the film shoot, with other people around. No, I'd do it that night, when we could meet and finally have some time alone.

There was just one problem. It happened when I got home that night, right after the film shoot. My parents were in the kitchen eating ribs from a bucket. Their fingers and faces were covered with barbecue sauce. I hadn't wanted to join them, but I did have to eat.

"Where were you?" my dad asked.

"What do you mean?" I said. "You know where I was. I was on the movie set."

"I don't mean that. I mean last night."

"Last night? You know that too. I was over at Gunnar's."

"Who else was over at Gunnar's?"

"What do you mean?" I was trying to evade the question again, but I was pretty sure where this was heading: my parents had learned about Otto. I guess their sources of information were moving faster now. It had taken them eight

months to learn that I was gay, but only three days to figure out that Otto was in town against their wishes.

My mom slapped the table. "Damn it, Russel! Tell us the truth!"

"Okay, okay," I said. Like I said, I didn't lie to my parents. "We'd been planning this visit for months," I went on. "But at the last minute, you say he can't stay here. Fine. Well, he *isn't* staying here. You didn't say he couldn't stay at Gunnar's. And even if you had, I don't see what business that is of yours."

My parents stood up from the table at exactly the same time.

"So you've been *seeing* him?" my mom said accusingly.

"Of course," I said.

"Russel, that is *not* acceptable!" my mom said.

"Like I said," I said, "I don't see what business that is of yours."

This probably wasn't the smartest thing to say. Whether it was their business or not, they could *make* it their business, since they were my parents.

Sure enough, my mom said, "Russel, you are *grounded*! You are not leaving this house for a month!"

In other words, I'd finally made a decision between Kevin and Otto—only now I couldn't be with either one!

CHAPTER NINE

COULD THERE POSSIBLY BE a worse time to be grounded?

But the thing is, I'd made my decision. I knew who I wanted to be with. I had to tell him. My parents thought they could stop that by grounding me? Well, in a nutshell, they were nuts.

I know I've said all along I was a good kid. But in this case, I simply had no choice except to sneak out of the house without their knowing.

Kevin. That's who I needed to see. I IMed him and told him to meet me at the stinky picnic gazebo. I also told him to give me a few minutes because I needed to build a dummy of myself out of clothes and put it under the covers of my bed. That way, if my parents peeked into my room, they

might think that I had gone to sleep early. I'd read about this in a book. I doubted it would work—it hadn't worked in the book!—but the consequences of my disobeying my parents and sneaking out the window were so harsh that I figured I should at least *try* to avoid them. Lucky for me, my bedroom was on the ground floor, so it was easy for me to sneak out the window.

My bike was in the garage, which was impossible to open without making a ruckus, so I had to run to the stinky picnic gazebo. I was out of breath by the time I got to the park. I could see the gazebo on the other side of the long soccer field. It looked smaller than I remembered, like a piece in some antique Christmas diorama.

Kevin was under the gazebo waiting for me. But there was someone with him—a guy with broad shoulders in some sort of overcoat. Was it his dad? I'd never seen a teenager dressed like that before. The acoustics of the park were strange, especially at night, and I could hear the mumble of them talking across that long expanse of lawn, but I couldn't make out anything they were saying.

Suddenly Kevin spotted me. He uttered something to the guy with him, who said something back, then hurried off into the woods.

What was this? I wondered.

I sprinted across the grass.

When I reached the gazebo, I immediately asked Kevin, "Who was that?" I was out of breath from all that running.

"Huh?" he said. He brushed away an insect.

"That guy I saw you talking to. Who was it? He looked older."

Kevin stared at me hard. "He *was* older," he said at last. He thought a moment more. "In his twenties. He was hitting on me. I've seen him here before."

I was thoroughly confused. "Kevin, what are you talking about? What do you mean you've 'seen' him here?"

Kevin slouched. "What do you *think*?"

Was Kevin saying what it sounded like he was saying? That he'd been out cruising the parks at night?

"Russel, relax," Kevin said. "I haven't done it that many times."

"'That many times'? Are you serious?" I admit it: Kevin was shocking me. We were standing under a gazebo, but *The Sound of Music* this wasn't. I thought I'd known him. Never in a million years would I have thought that he'd be out in parks at night with guys (other than me, I mean).

Suddenly Kevin was impatient. "Look! What'd you want to see me about?"

"Well, I'm confused," I said. "Last week you were all moony-eyed over me. You came out to the whole school so we could be together. Now you tell me you've been out picking up old guys in parks?"

Kevin shrugged, but it was really more of a squirm. "Well, it's not like we were together then. And it's not like that has anything to do with us anyway. That's just sex."

"Kevin!"

"*What?*"

I didn't know what to say. Was it possible that I had misjudged him so thoroughly? Last summer, before I'd gotten together with Otto, I'd fallen in love with a guy at camp who I'd thought was perfect. And he had turned out to be a complete creep.

But Kevin wasn't a creep. Was he? True, I'd known that he was weak—that when push came to shove, he did the easy thing. He'd come out at school, but eight months too late, and probably only to get my attention anyway. And that guy Kevin had been with at the movie shoot? Maybe he hadn't been hitting on Kevin—maybe Kevin had been hitting on *him.*

"You know," Kevin said, "this is getting to be a real bore. When did you get such a stick up your butt?"

I was speechless. I *had* been wrong about him, just like

I'd been wrong about that guy at camp. *Boy*, was Kevin weak! He couldn't even wait for me in a park without getting it on with another guy? I suddenly felt like I had with my parents when they'd confronted me about being gay, like he was pulling off a human mask to reveal the true monster underneath.

"So it was all lies?" I said. "When you said you still loved me? You were just messing around?"

He squirmed again, like a man in a straitjacket. "Hey, I'm an athlete. It's a game. And this was one game I wanted to win. I lost the first time around, so I wanted a rematch. I wanted to prove I could win. And I did. I got you to pick me over Otto. But that's all it was. Just a game."

I didn't answer. The truth was, I hadn't picked him. I'd picked Otto. That's what had been so obvious when I'd stared in that mirror at school, when I'd seen the reflection of that zombie glaring back at me. Being a zombie was about being dead, about the past, about a life already lived. Kevin was about the past too. He and I had had our chance, but that moment was gone. We couldn't go back—everything was different now. Being human, being a high school student, that was about the future, about promise, about all the life yet to be lived. It was exactly like Declan McDonnell had said. I didn't have a jeweled dagger like Brad, the hero

of the movie, but Declan McDonnell had given me the insight I needed to vanquish the past once and for all. The right choice for me was the guy who represented a new life, and the future—Otto, no matter the difficulties.

I'd come here to tell Kevin that he and I really were over. I'd wanted to tell him before I said anything to Otto, because I didn't want any unfinished business when I finally laid it on the line with him. I was choosing Otto with all my heart and soul, and if he didn't want me anymore, fine. I didn't want to keep Kevin as sort of a fall-back boyfriend.

But I didn't tell Kevin any of this. What was the point now, since I was never going to talk to him again? In a way, I was grateful. Because he had made it completely clear that by picking Otto, I had absolutely positively made the *right* choice.

"Good-bye, Kevin," I said, and I turned to go.

"Yeah, whatever," he mumbled.

And so I just walked away. It wasn't like the last time I'd left him behind in this gazebo, when I really had been torn, looking back at him as I went.

Still, when I reached the opposite side of the soccer field, I did look back. I couldn't believe it! Kevin was already back in the arms of the old guy in the overcoat. I'd

thought the man had run away, but he hadn't. He must have been hiding in the bushes all the while, listening to Kevin and me. Now he and Kevin were hugging, and probably kissing. Kevin was even weaker than I'd thought.

I couldn't watch. I hurried away. It was the funniest thing, though. As I reached the street at the edge of the park, I swear I heard the sound of someone sobbing. It echoed out above the grass. I couldn't see Kevin anymore, but I knew it couldn't have been him anyway, because of the way he'd acted. I figured it was just the strange acoustics of the park — that someone in one of the surrounding houses was crying in a bedroom with the window open.

I went straight to Gunnar's house.

"Oh!" he said when he opened the door.

"Is Otto here?" I said. "I really need to talk to him."

He flashed me a grin. "Oh, good! I was hoping you'd pick him!" I hadn't meant to let him know the reason I'd come, but somehow Gunnar had seen it on my face.

Otto stepped into the hallway behind Gunnar.

"Hi," I said.

"Hi," he said.

"Want to go for a walk? I have something I want to tell you."

"Sure," he said. "Let me get my coat."

As we were waiting, Gunnar leaned forward and whispered, "Don't worry about ticks, Russ. If you get any, they're really not that big a deal."

We didn't go anywhere near the stinky picnic gazebo. That had been the place for Kevin and me. (And I definitely didn't want to run into Kevin and his new "friend"!) Meanwhile, the place for Otto and me was a moonlit lake way up in the mountains. So, thinking we needed some new romantic spot, I took Otto to a different lake—really more of a pond—on the outskirts of town. I'd played there as a kid, but I'd never been there in the dark.

It looked completely different at night, all soft-focus and muted lighting, like the Rivendell scenes in the movie version of *The Lord of the Rings*. It was as if we'd stepped right into the reflection on the surface of the pond, and everything around us was silver and shimmering. The cattail fronds glowed, and above us, the stars and moon seemed to ripple in the air. Surrounding us, a ring of trees, their bare branches protectively intertwined, shielded us from the outside world. The air was clean and wet, and I could smell Otto's musk as

well, even from five feet away. It may have been another swamp, but there was no hint of methane here.

"Otto," I said as we walked. "I just wanted to say I'm sorry."

"I knew it," he said. "You're breaking up with me, aren't you?"

"Huh? No. No!" I stopped him. "That's not it at all." I took a breath. "I just wanted to say I'm sorry for being distant these last couple of days. It was just something I needed to figure out. But it was stupid, because you came all this way, and we only had this short time together." I figured there was no reason to tell him about Kevin because (a) it was probably kind of obvious what had been going on with me, and (b) that was all over now anyway.

"You're not breaking up with me?" Otto said. Like the pond, he looked different in the moonlight—lighter, a white marble statue come to life. His scar made half of the statue look rough, unfinished.

"Nope," I said. "You're not getting rid of me that easy. But I did want to talk about what we do next."

"What do you mean?"

I explained how I was grounded right then, and that even if my parents didn't find out I'd snuck out without their permission, they were going to do everything they could to keep him and me apart. As hard as it would be to

see each other under normal circumstances, my parents were going to make it much, much harder.

"They might not even let me go to camp next summer," I said. "They know that's where we met. They could even send me to one of those 'ex-gay' camps instead. That's how nuts they are about this."

"Damn, Russel, I'm sorry."

"Screw 'em! I love you, that's all that matters. But I wanted to let you know all this, and ask if you still wanted to be with me."

Otto rolled his eyes. "Of course I do."

I stepped forward and kissed him. The moment my lips touched his, I was once again living in my skin—the skin on my body, and the "skin" that somehow contained my aura or soul. When we'd kissed before, it had felt like our souls were touching, but tonight I wasn't sure where his soul ended and mine began. Same for his mouth and tongue. I finally knew what they meant when they talk about lovers becoming one.

"So what do we do?" I said, later. It may have been ten minutes, or it might have been an hour—I wasn't sure. "How do we make this work?"

"I'm not worried," he said. "We'll just have to get creative."

We stayed near that pond for a long time. In fact, I didn't get home until almost 5 A.M. After all, we only had this one night together in who knows how long?

What did we do in all that time? Let's just say Otto and I made the most of our time together, and leave it at that.

CHAPTER TEN

OTTO WENT HOME THE next day. I couldn't go with him to the airport, which sucked, but we'd said our good-byes the night before.

My parents actually bought the dummy-thing. That meant there was at least one bright side to the whole situation with them: they were smart, but not so smart that I couldn't somehow keep seeing Otto on the sly.

That Sunday, we had a meeting in the family room.

"We're very disappointed with you, Russel," my mom said. "Very, very disappointed."

Well, I'm very disappointed with both of you, I wanted to say. Very, very disappointed. So I guess we were even.

"As long as you're living in our house," my mom went on, "you're going to have to live by our rules."

How have I not lived by your rules? I wanted to ask. They'd said Otto couldn't stay at their house, and so I'd made other arrangements—despite how unreasonable my parents' demand really was. It sounded to me like they didn't just want me living by their rules. It sounded to me like they didn't want me to be gay.

"We're a family," my mom said. "And somehow we have to learn to get along. So we're all going to have to make sacrifices."

Let me guess, I wanted to say: your sacrifice will be the almost unbearable burden of having a gay son. And my sacrifice will be to stop seeing Otto (or any other boy, ever, for that matter).

But I didn't say this either.

My mom and I stared at each other. I knew what she was thinking, but I don't think she had any idea what I was thinking. That's the thing about gay people and straight people. We gay people understand them a lot better than they understand us. After all, we *have* to understand them, in order to live. But most straight people don't even *try* to understand us. They have no reason to.

Finally, I said, "Fine. We'll all make sacrifices."

I knew as soon as I said it that this was the truth. I *was* going to be making a sacrifice, but not the one my parents

thought. Oh, I was definitely going to go right on seeing Otto, which was my right as a human being. But now I was going to have to lie about it to my parents. In a way, they were just as much about the past as Kevin was. And if I was going to embrace my new future with Otto, I was going to have to vanquish them too. But in this case, my weapon of choice was going to be little white lies.

Anyway, that meant my relationship with my parents was changing, maybe forever. They were still my parents, and I loved them. But I wasn't a child. They still had some say in my life, but not about this. In this case, they were dead wrong. So I guess that's what I was sacrificing: some of my faith in them, and maybe even what was left of my childhood.

But later, to my surprise, my dad knocked on my door.

"What," I said.

He stuck his head inside and said, "Can I talk to you for a minute?"

I was sitting at my computer. I nodded.

He came in and sat on the bed. Suddenly his hands were just the most fascinating things to him. He smelled like Lavoris and Parmesan cheese.

"Russel," he said awkwardly. "I just wanted to say that I know how hard this must be for you."

"You do?" I said. I admit it, I was totally surprised.

He nodded. "And I wanted to talk about your mother too."

"What about her?" I said warily.

"She loves you, Russel. Very, very much."

Oh, sure, I thought. She "loves" me—just so long as I conform to her image of exactly who I'm "supposed" to be.

"She'll come aound," my dad said. "She doesn't think she can, but I know she will. She loves you too much not too. But I wanted to ask a favor of you. She doesn't know I'm asking, and it's not fair of me to ask you. It's not fair of her to need me to ask you. She's not perfect. Then again, who is?"

"What favor?" I said.

142 "Give her some time."

I thought about this for a second. Then before I knew it, I found myself nodding. "Yeah," I said. "I can give her some time."

Was it just possible, I thought, however unlikely, that my parents weren't quite the terrible monsters that I had made them out to be?

Sunday night, Min stopped by. I guess my mom hadn't yet heard that she was bi, because she let Min come in and see me, despite my being grounded. (Or maybe my mom thought that, Min being bi, there was still a chance she and

I could get together!)

"So," Min said.

"So," I said. I felt bad that I'd been keeping her in the dark lately—that I'd just assumed she would somehow judge me if I'd told her the truth about Kevin and Otto.

So I told her everything.

She listened to it all, but there was something not quite right about her reactions. I couldn't put my finger on it, but it was almost like she'd heard it before. Maybe Gunnar had filled her in.

Finally, when I was done, she said, "You've had a busy couple of weeks."

"Yeah," I said. "Sorry I haven't kept you up-to-date."

"Here's the thing. I haven't exactly kept you up-to-date either."

"You haven't?"

Min nodded guiltily. "Girl problems. It's a pretty complicated story."

"What girl?" I said. "When was this? I had no idea!"

"That's funny, because if it weren't for you, there would be no story."

"Really? Why's that?"

So Min told me. And I have to say, she was absolutely right.

I also realized that I wasn't nearly as observant as I'd thought.

Monday at school, Min, Gunnar, and I were walking down the hallway, and we came across that poster calling for extras for *Attack of the Soul-Sucking Brain Zombies*—the one that had started this whole thing in the first place. It was out-of-date now, but no one had taken it down. As for the movie itself, there were still more scenes to be done with the extras, but I was grounded, so I wouldn't be going.

"Damn," I said. "Something just occurred to me." I turned to Min. "I owe you ten bucks."

"What?" she said.

"Don't you remember? When we first saw this poster? You bet that if we did the movie, we'd all have completely different experiences?"

"Yeah," mumbled Gunnar. "*Someone* was in a bad mood that day."

"The fact is," I said, "you were right." I thought about everything that had happened—my encounters with Kevin, Declan McDonnell, and Otto, not to mention all the crap with my parents. "*Boy*, were you right! Talk about completely different experiences!" I reached for my wallet.

Min stopped me. "It's okay. I didn't win that bet."

I looked up at her.

"Sure, different things happened to each of us," she said. "But we were together too, in more ways than one. Even when we weren't together, we were together, you know?"

I thought about this. I remembered Thanksgiving dinner, and how comforting it had felt to be surrounded by such good friends. And I thought about how nice it had been for Min and me to finally share our different experiences with each other. So I guess Min had a point.

"Oh," I said to Min. "Well, in that case, you can pay *me*!"

Min laughed. Gunnar did too.

"No," I said. "Seriously! Pay up!"

Only now did I join in their laughter. If you can't laugh when you're grounded for a month, when can you laugh?

"So what's next?" Gunnar said.

"What do you mean?" Min asked.

"Oh, you know us," Gunnar said. "Seems like we're always in the middle of something. So what's next?"

I had plenty of ideas, but being grounded, I wouldn't be getting to them anytime soon. Besides, you can't go on and on in life, never stopping, never resting. Every now and then, it's a good idea to take a little breather and say, That part of my life is over, and for the time being, we've come to . . .

THE END

Or is it?

Or is it?